SHATTERED
Wonderland

SHATTERED *Wonderland*

THE *Lucent* CHRONICLES #2

Published by

TWO REALMS PUBLISHING LLC

HTTPS://TWO-REALMS-PUBLISHING-LLC.COM/

ISBN: 978-1-955106-42-9

Cover and Interior Design: We Got You Covered Book Design

Editor: Michelle's Edits

Printed in the United States of America

THE
Lucent
CHRONICLES

SHATTERED
Wonderland

BRIGIT ROSÉ

Welcome to Wonder, where right side up is upside down, north is south, east is west, and the only thing that makes sense is that nothing makes sense.

Because here, we're all mad.

And a little dirty.

CHAPTER *one*

Alicia spun on the back of her heel as she peered down the hallway. Where had the voice come from? No one should be upstairs. The whispers continued, forcing her feet to move as if she was a puppet. How was that even possible? What was going on? Maybe if she tracked the noise to its source, she'd get some answers. The thick carpet silenced her steps as she strode forward. She stopped just outside her father's study. Was this right? Pressing her ear against the oak door, she listened for the voice.

"You're mine," it commanded.

"What the…?" she muttered under her breath. Her blonde hair whipped back as she glanced over her shoulder. The hallway remained blessedly empty. Quietly, Alicia slipped into the study. Her father mostly used it, but she kept a few items… collectibles on various shelves. Stepping farther into the room, she scrutinized the different bookcases and display cases. Nothing jumped out at her.

Out of her periphery, she glimpsed a flash of white. She chased after it and skidded to a halt in front of the fireplace. A yellow egg inlaid with Austrian crystals sat atop the mantel. It was the music box her grandmother had gifted her this past Yule. Her father insisted that an enchanted item like it was safer in his study. Not that he'd given her much choice in the matter.

Something that seemed to be as much a part of her legacy as her powers. None of it was in her control. Though she was determined to prove her family otherwise. Scrutinizing the sparkling stones, Alicia canted her head. They seemed to shine brighter than she'd seen over the last month. Except that made no sense. Of all the days she'd spent studying the egg, why now? What was so different about today?

"There you are," her sister's voice rang out. "I've been looking everywhere for you."

Biting back a groan, Alicia's attention snapped to the doorway. She glanced back at the egg. It appeared perfectly normal. *Great,* she thought to herself. Just when she might actually get some answers regarding the egg's enchantment, someone interrupted her focus. "What can I do for you, Angel?"

"We need to get you ready for the party. Mother and I selected a beautiful blue chiffon dress for you."

Alicia let out a heavy sigh and narrowed her gaze at her sister. Tonight was supposed to be special. Her idea of special meant her family allowed her to choose her own path. Which would've included grappling the spell placed on the egg. Something she was so close to attaining. If only they'd given her a few more minutes. "Can't I just skip the party?"

"No, but you know that." Angel clasped her hands in front of her body. "I've been where you are. I know it's a lot, but we have a legacy to live up to."

Right. The female had met her husband only a few years ago, just after her twenty-third birthday. Alicia crossed her arms. Now that she had turned twenty-three, her family expected her to follow the same antiquated tradition. *Lilith, help me,* she silently pleaded. "That doesn't mean I have to look forward to it."

"Heath will make a wonderful husband for you." Her sister offered her a warm smile. "Now, come on. Let's get you ready."

Rubbing her forehead, she cocked an eyebrow at Angel. In what world did that make sense? "Well, I suppose he's just as good as the next self-absorbed asshole." That didn't mean she wanted to marry him. If only her family could understand that. Alicia let out a heavy sigh. "Let's just get this over with."

"I'm not sure that's the attitude to have, but I'll take it. As long as you promise to be polite during the actual party."

"It isn't exactly like I have a choice," she mumbled. Although, if she rejected any offers or caused the man to walk away, did that mean she wouldn't have to go through with anything? It was certainly something to consider. How upset would her parents be? Or would they merely express disappointment? Or force her into it, anyway? That seemed more aligned to their standards.

Angel gathered Alicia's hands in her own. "Listen to me. None of this is as bad as you're making it out to be. We all have our part in our faction. Marrying Heath could be just what you need to strengthen not only our family, but your powers, too. Isn't that what you want?"

Not in the least. She wanted to discover her own inner strength. Something that existed somewhere. Alicia peered over her shoulder at the egg on the mantel. She just hadn't figured out where to look. Or how to find it. Her gaze returned to her sister. "What if I decline his offer? What then?"

"I don't know. You'd have to discuss that with Father."

That wasn't what she hoped to hear. The man hadn't considered her feelings before. Why would tonight make a difference? Maybe she'd get lucky and the Frost faction wouldn't show. Or the agreement would blow up. Wouldn't that be something? Alicia smirked. "Knowing my luck, something is bound to go wrong."

"If you keep thinking like that, it will." Angel frowned. "Can we please go get dressed now?"

"Yeah. Let's go." Maybe that was exactly how she needed to think. Then it would come to pass, giving her the one thing she truly wanted—freedom. Absolute freedom. Nothing more, nothing less. Just freedom and everything that came with it. Didn't that just bring a smile to her face?

The creature snapped its jaw at him. Lewis jumped back before its gnarly teeth latched onto his arm. His gaze flicked to the sword tucked between its front and hind legs. He needed to get the damn thing back. Not that he could do that from his current position.

Fucking worebeore. Between its claws, teeth, spiked fur, and height, it had all the advantage. It stood at least a couple of feet taller than him. In this form, anyway. If he shifted, then he had a better chance of retrieving his weapon.

As it was his only way out of this fucking nightmare, he had no other choice. Unless… Lewis feigned a step to the left. The creature swiped at him, forcing him to leap back. *Shit.* That was too close. He had no other option. Shifting to his animal form would even things out.

A small smirk played at the corner of his lips as another idea popped into his head. One he liked even better than the first. Too many found jackrabbits less than threatening. Despite his size, he didn't believe this would be any different. His human form didn't hinder him. It just offered another solution, especially with a creature that was all brawn and no brain.

Lewis stole a glimpse over his shoulder as he backed up toward the treeline behind him. It wasn't too far out of reach. Then he'd only require one move to knock the worebeore down and grab his sword.

A low growl rumbled out of the creature as it stalked him, leaving the weapon forgotten on the ground. Drool dribbled from its mouth. Its tongue swept across its gaping maw. The worebeore stared at him hungrily, almost as if he could be its next meal.

That definitely wasn't fucking happening. Lewis glanced back. They were almost—he jumped back just as the worebeore swiped its claw at him. Refusing to wait another second, he leaped toward the closest tree. He pushed against the trunk with the bottom of his boot, increasing the power behind his left hook. His fist connected with the side of the worebeore's head.

The creature stumbled and fell on its side. It shook its head, taking a moment to gather its bearings, and slowly clambered to its paws.

This was his chance. Lewis darted around the worebeore, sidestepping it, and grabbed his blade. Just as his fingers wrapped around the sword's hilt, the worebeore's tail whipped against him and sent him flying. He sailed through the air and slammed into a tree trunk with a thud. "Fuck," he grunted.

Burning pain speared his shoulder. Spots flashed in his field of vison. His heart thundered in his chest. His lungs constricted, making it difficult to breathe. *Shit.* What the fuck was happening to him? He shook his head to pull himself together. Had this place finally driven him insane? He scrubbed a hand across his face and took in slow, shallow breaths. The stinging in his body eased. Everything around him settled. That hurt more than he expected.

The creature had come around way too soon. At least he'd gotten his sword back. Now, he just had to keep a hold of it and himself. Not that it would help him win against the worebeore. As much as he loathed the idea of running, he had to fight smarter, not harder. Scanning his surroundings, Lewis located a small hollow nearby. He could hide there. Just long enough to gather his bearings and come up with a plan. One that got him closer to escape, because he had to get the fuck out of this place.

Before he really lost it.

Lewis surveyed the distance between him and the hollow. He eyed the several gnarled roots and twisted branches he'd have to climb over and around. They burrowed into the ground like a sea of mufflers. The corner of his mouth lifted as a pattern revealed itself to him. Without a second thought, he raced toward the hiding spot.

He could make it.

For his own survival, he had to.

Surveying the room, Alicia tipped her glass back and sipped more wine. Goddess, she needed it to get through this evening. Her supposed betrothed prattled on about something. She'd stopped tracking his words a few minutes ago, possibly longer. Although she should pay attention, her mind constantly wandered back to the music box.

What if what she'd heard was a clue that might help her break the enchantment? Was it possible? Perhaps. She'd have to consult her family's grimoire for that. Although she had a few of her own spell books, none of them compared to their family's book. It contained every spell that anyone in their ancestral line had ever cast. If there was a way to break the egg's enchantment, she'd locate it in there. Except both her grandmother and father refused to grant her access to it.

"Don't you agree, Alicia?" Heath asked.

Her gaze jerked in his direction. *Shit.* She really should have paid attention. Now, she either looked like a sacrificial animal or acted as if she agreed with whatever pretentious comment he'd made. Goddess, she wished his thick accent didn't grind her nerves so much. It reminded her of a squealing pig. Then maybe she would've heard what he uttered.

A soft melody sounded around her. Alicia's eyes narrowed as she scanned her surroundings. Where had that come from? It sounded different from the piano, gently playing in the background. She eyed the three patrons that stood nearby, eagerly awaiting her response.

The melody chimed again.

Without giving an answer, she walked away and followed the song she heard. It was like some tether she couldn't refuse. Alicia exited the party room. She stopped just outside the entrance and lingered in the hallway, listening intently for the song to make itself known. Maybe she simply needed to pick a direction. She glanced one way and then the other.

The most angelic sound she'd ever heard rang out, almost as if it called to her. Strange. It came from upstairs. The urge to seek it out was so strong she couldn't ignore it. She set her nearly empty wine glass down on a side table, continued down the hall, rounded the corner, and headed up the staircase. The stairs creaked beneath her feet with each step she took as she made her ascent.

Beckoned by the melody, she continued toward it as she hit the second-floor landing. It led her right back to her father's study. *Did that mean?* Could the music box have called out to her? That seemed impossible, except… it had an enchantment on it.

Alicia glanced in both directions down the hallway. Maybe she was wrong. The song rang out again. The train of her dress trailed behind her as she stopped in front of the study. She gripped the doorknob and hesitated. What would she find on the other side of the door? What if this was just a trick? One set to destroy everything her family had built over the centuries.

She peered over her shoulder, scrutinizing the portraits hanging along the wall as if they offered an answer. Each one depicted a great matriarch of her family. They were one of a few factions that could trace their line back to Lilith. A powerful witch who overcame every obstacle placed at her feet. Someone who paved their own path. Just like she yearned to do. She couldn't allow her family to hold her back.

Nodding to herself, Alicia opened the door and slipped inside the study. As she eased the door shut, she surveyed the room. Nothing appeared out of place. It all looked just as she'd left it an hour earlier. The pot of ink and quill still sat atop the large oak desk to her left. Books lined the various shelves of the floor-to-ceiling bookcases in front of her. The yellow egg inlaid with Austrian crystals rested atop the mantel.

A haunting note filled the room. It sounded like a heavy beat or… like something galloped… toward her. She backed up a step. It got louder. Her eyes widened as she stepped farther back, nearly bumping into the desk. The noise came from behind her, darting across the room. She spun around on the back of her heel. A fire burst free in the fireplace. Flames licked at the brick, charring the edges.

Sparkling light emanated from the egg. Its shadow danced across the dark carpet, reaching out toward her. A flash of white sprinted in her direction. It circled her feet and wound around her, caressing her skin like a lover. Then it took off, tugging her along toward the crackling flames. She fought against it; its hold only strengthened. Her hand shot out to the mantel. She gripped it tightly, struggling against the light as it threatened to drag her into the fire.

The door flew open.

The flames disappeared. Silence filled the room. The light from the egg completely dissipated. Alicia's eyes darted around the study. Everything looked normal, as if nothing had ever happened. Her heart beat loudly in her chest. Ragged breaths left her mouth. *What the fuck?* Had her mind played a trick on her? No. That wasn't possible. She'd seen it, felt the claws across her flesh as the light clung to her.

"Alicia? Are you okay?"

Her gaze snapped to her grandmother's face. *That's a damn good question.* What the hell had she seen? Felt? What happened? "I don't know," she muttered and peered at the egg. Maybe she couldn't explain what had occurred, but she was positive it had done something.

"Talk to me, my dear. What is churning in that mind of yours?"

Alicia scrubbed a hand across her face. She chewed on the inside of her cheek. Although her grandmother understood her better than anyone else, she didn't think it was wise to share what tumbled around in her head. That didn't mean she couldn't take advantage of this moment. "Where did you get this egg, Grandma?"

"Grace with *Olde Time Trinkets* found it for me. Why do you ask?"

That didn't tell her much. She'd heard stories regarding the female and that shop. It was the place to go for strange and unusual items. Not that she'd ever visited. Maybe now she had a reason to go. Staring at the egg, she folded her arms across her chest and half-shrugged. "I guess I'm just trying to figure this piece out. The more I know, the easier I can…" her words trailed off. They'd discussed the enchantment once before. It seemed pointless to bring it up again.

"You're not strong enough to break the enchantment. I told you, a powerful witch placed it."

Her head swiveled in her grandmother's direction. Her whole life, she'd heard endless complaints about her lack of control and strength. Yes, her spells fizzled out, but that didn't make her incompetent. "Then why'd you get it for me?" Alicia snapped. She hadn't meant for the question to come out that way, but why didn't anyone in her family have faith in her?

"I believe it will set you on your path." Her grandmother let out a heavy sigh, strode across the room, and squeezed Alicia's forearm. "I'm not saying you'll never break it. Just that it'll take time for you to get there." The female pointed a wrinkled finger at the egg. "This is a special piece, Alicia. While I didn't tell Grace exactly what I was looking for, when she presented this to me, I knew it was meant for you. And only you."

"Only me? How could you know that? Did Grace tell you where she got it from?" The more she learned about the egg, the larger the mystery it held. It just made her even more determined to solve it. This music box had attempted twice now to reach out to her. Did that make her grandmother right? It was meant for her.

"No. Grace has… a unique ability. Her own kind of magic. Not like ours. She's shapeshifter kin, so it links more to them, but offers her insight into our world. The moment I laid my hands on this music box, something inside of me stirred and I got an image of you in my head. That's how I knew it belonged to you."

Okay. At least part of that made sense. Sort of. Her gaze narrowed. "I thought we're not supposed to interact with shapeshifters… of any kind." That's how her parents had raised her. To her, it seemed like an asinine law. Hunters killed all manner of supernatural creatures. It made more sense that they worked together, not fought one another.

"Oh, posh. That law doesn't regard shopping. Besides, she's only kin. I have only seen one shifter around there, and he was another patron."

Pursing her lips, she bit the inside of her cheek and gazed at the egg. Did that mean Grace knew something about the music box? Had the female recognized it as enchanted? "Does Grace know what you are?"

"No. I don't believe so." A warm smile crossed her grandmother's face. "Now, I know you're determined to solve this puzzle, and I believe you will. Just not tonight. Come, let us return to the party."

Gods, that was the theme for the night. A celebration for her and her betrothed. Alicia rolled her eyes. "He's such a tool, Grandma. What *if* my path takes me anywhere but to Heath?"

"Then that is the direction you were meant to go. You'll never know that if you don't at least give him a chance."

A chance? How much more of herself did she have to give the guy? She'd clung to his side most of the night and pretended to hang on to his every word. No matter how much she'd ignored him, she had acted like the good fiancée. "What if I've done all of that?"

"Have you?" Her grandmother raised an eyebrow. "I know you, Alicia. You're as stubborn as I was at your age. I promise Heath is a good match. You'll never see the truth if you don't make a valid attempt."

Right. Something she hadn't actually done. That didn't make her blind. She just saw the truth easier than others in her family. Maybe she needed to give them the opportunity to see it for themselves. A slight smirk settled on her face as the corner of her mouth upturned. "Alright, Grandma. I just need another minute to collect myself and then I'll rejoin the party."

"But of course. Don't take too long." With a dip of her chin, her grandmother exited the study.

Alicia waited until the female disappeared down the staircase before she moved. She only had one chance to get her family to understand her truth. To show them all she could make her own path. Something beyond the small shop and apartment she'd carved out for herself. Grabbing the egg, she raced across the room to her father's desk. She quickly located the skeleton key he kept in the top drawer.

Maybe her spell books hadn't held the answer. Nor had the music box's origin. That left her one place to look. Silently closing the drawer, she slipped the key into the pocket of her dress and turned toward the back bookcase. Alicia gently pulled on the thick Lewis Carroll book. With a faint creak, the case swung outward. She glanced over her shoulder and slipped into the hidden passage.

The door drifted shut behind her. Clutching the egg against her body, she descended the cold, stone staircase. Hopefully, her family understood why she left. She couldn't keep pretending. This was her life, and she had to be true to herself. Consequences be damned.

CHAPTER
Two

LEWIS PRESSED HIS back tighter against the hollow he'd burrowed himself inside of. Although silence greeted him, he knew the worebeore remained out there. It simply bided its time, crawling through the forest and around the ancient, timeless trees, rough with age. Leaves on the ground didn't even crunch beneath its paws. That didn't mean it had left. Though he wished it did.

A feminine voice rang out around him.

"What the fuck?" he mumbled. That was impossible. Unless… no. The creature wouldn't have summoned the Red Queen. That female never left the comforts of her fortress.

It sounded out again, chanting something in a language he didn't understand.

That definitely wasn't the Red Queen. The voice sounded softer, more melodic than anything he'd ever heard. Shivers shot down his spine. Shaking the sensation off, he inched forward and peered out from the hollow.

Maybe it came from the dancing roses. No. This was the Whispering Woods. Not Fogley Forest. Those creatures were too far away for him to hear anything from them. Even the wind couldn't carry their song this far. Besides, he'd spent enough time in Wonder to recognize every language.

"Keep your head out and you might lose it."

His eyes snapped to the blue-and-purple-striped cat floating in the air mere feet from where he stood. "Holloway. What are you doing here?"

"Saving you, of course." The creature snickered.

"Like any of your advice has helped over the years," Lewis retorted. He'd lost track of how long he'd been stuck in this hellhole. All he knew anymore was that he desperately needed to escape.

"You are still alive, are you not?"

That meant little in the long run. Yes, his heart still physically beat, but this place had shredded his soul into a thousand pieces. If he didn't escape soon, the rest wouldn't fucking matter. Sneering, Lewis peered across the dense forest. Although the sun had set over an hour ago, a flash of light broke through the lush canopy. It penetrated the leaves, casting an unearthly golden luminescence across the ground. His entire body straightened as his fingers tightened around the hilt of the sword he held.

"Go now," the cat hissed.

"What?" His gaze narrowed at Holloway. Hadn't the cat just warned him against leaving? Now the creature *wanted* him to go. What the fuck?

"Go now or you will miss it."

"Miss what?" None of this made a lick of sense. To make matters worse, the cat rotated its body and slowly disappeared. "Miss what, Holloway?" This fucking thing couldn't leave without giving him some kind of answer.

"Your freedom."

Those two words rang out loudly in his ears as the cat vanished from sight. Without a second thought, Lewis ran from the comfort of the hollow and raced toward the light. He didn't know what awaited his arrival, but it was better than what he left behind.

Alicia grunted as she pushed up onto her hands and knees. Sitting up, she surveyed her surroundings. Where the hell was she? What the hell happened? One second, she recited a spell from the book… "Shit!" She patted the ground fervently, shoved dead leaves out of the way, and scoured the nearby bushes. Nothing. Where the hell could it have ended up? "Shit, shit, shit."

It had to be here somewhere. Not that she had a clue where she'd ended up. Unless… Alicia spun around in circles as she stared down various parts of a lush forest. No. It wasn't possible. Except, it was the only thing that made sense. Somehow, she'd fallen into the egg. While she had managed to half-catch herself, she was still inside of some world attached to the damn thing.

"This isn't happening." She gripped the back of her neck. No one in her family would find her here. Especially as she'd left the party without so much as a word. Or her phone. And attempted to break the egg's enchantment at a park. Witches avoided parks because of the shifters.

"Run," a voice stated behind her.

Alicia spun on the back of her heel, staggered backward, and nearly tripped over a large root in the ground. *Shit.* Her eyes widened at the fat, blue-and-purple-striped floating cat. Had the warning just come from it? It could have. Kind of like a familiar. "What?"

"Run," he repeated.

As strange as it was, she wasn't the type of person to ignore a warning like that a second time. Especially from a cat that reminded her of her grandmother's familiar, Duchess. Picking a random direction, Alicia lifted the skirting of her dress and ran. At least as best as she could. Stiletto high heels weren't conducive to the soft ground.

A clopping sound reverberated through the trees not far behind her. She glanced over her shoulder at the noise. *Holy shit.* Some large bear-like creature charged after her with several soldiers hot on its trail. Focusing on the dense sea of green plant life, Alicia pushed herself and ran harder than should be possible in the shoes she wore.

That cat had completely disappeared. It hadn't given her any insight on how to escape, but there had to be a way out. Or at least somewhere to hide from those that chased her. She refused to die here.

Her heart raced and her lungs burned with each step she took. She drank in her surroundings as her feet pounded against the earth. At least what she could, anyway. Shrubbery blurred into an endless body of green. It all blended together. Alicia couldn't tell north from south. Even if she could, she didn't know which way she ran, but slowing down wasn't an option.

Fuck. This wasn't supposed to happen. She'd gone to the park with one goal—break the enchantment. Not get sucked into it. Where had it all gone wrong?

Alicia flipped the page, skimming another spell in the grimoire. She'd already attempted three others and none of them worked. The egg still sat there and sparkled in complete contrast to the grassy area she'd chosen to work. Something had to give. This entire endeavor couldn't be for naught.

With a heavy sigh, she turned to a different page. It looked the same as all the others. Useless. Alicia groaned. "Come on. Think. There's got to be something in here." She chewed on the inside of her cheek. Maybe she needed to go about this differently. Getting to her feet, she set the grimoire on the ground, picked up the small steel blade, and sliced her palm. Holding the egg in one hand, she squeezed her other hand. Droplets of blood fell, landing on the egg and grimoire. "Clavem quaerite," Alicia chanted repeatedly.

The third time the words left her mouth, a heavy breeze ruffled her dress. The wind sped up, swirling around her. It tore through the grimoire's pages, rapidly shuffling through them. Her fingers prickled, and she dropped the egg.

Maybe that was it. She'd let go of the egg, which struck the—a hand covered her mouth. Someone dragged her backward. She struggled against their grip and elbowed them in the gut.

"Stop it," a rough masculine voice whispered in her ear. Tingles shot down her spine. "You want to stay alive?"

The hairs on the back of her neck rose. Had she run right into a deathtrap? Shit. Given her track record, it seemed highly plausible. No. She refused to die in this place. Maybe if she summoned a little fire, she could distract this guy and run away. Not that she was great at earth magic. Right then, playing along made the most sense. Her gut twisted as she nodded.

"Then do as I say." His hold eased a bit as he slowly let go of her. "And maybe we'll both get the fuck out of here."

Alicia eyed their immediate surroundings. She needed a suitable spot to ignite a small fire. Something that would draw this guy's attention long enough for her to escape. A smile pile of gold and red leaves not ten feet away seemed like an excellent option. Though the large root just opposite of it might be better. As the male fully released her out of his grip, she flicked her wrist. A spark flickered across the bark, but it appeared like nothing more than a tiny flash of light. *Damn it.* That wasn't enough.

Her gaze flicked to the man who'd grabbed her. Warmth flooded her body as her gaze landed on his ruggedly handsome face. His golden-brown eyes narrowed at her. His plump lips pinched together in a thin line. Her heart thumped loudly, ticking in her ears like an overwound clock. She swallowed to wet her parched throat. Who the hell was this guy? Where had he come from?

Turning slightly, Alicia studied him closely. Maybe with some insight, she could answer some of her own questions. She watched as he scratched at his five o'clock shadow and ran a hand through his frizzy, chestnut-brown hair. A few stray curls hung loosely across his forehead. Her fingers wiggled against her hip. She had this unexplainable itch to run them through his hair. Goddess, what the fuck was wrong with her? She needed to learn more about him, but not like this.

Shaking the sensation from her body, she focused on the male. He stood a foot taller than her, possibly more. His body was lean and muscular. Nothing like the males she'd grown up around. They were all sinewy. None of them filled out a sleeveless tunic like the male who stood before her. The thin material stretched across his broad shoulders as he folded his arms across his sculpted chest. She glimpsed a tattoo of a heart with a tilted crown on his right biceps. And another tattoo on his left forearm. Though she could only make out an outline of a skeleton, a crown, and a handlebar. Was that a motorcycle? Alicia gripped her shoulder. She seriously needed to stop staring. "What are we waiting for? Shouldn't we be running?" Or doing something besides standing here doing nothing except gawking at one another.

He raised an eyebrow at her, but he said nothing. Not far off, a loud thud resounded and a whimpered roar followed. The male gestured toward the noise. "Let's go." He spun around on the back of his heel and took off.

Alicia blinked and trailed behind him. Gods, she prayed, he was the answer she needed. She didn't know what she'd do if he wasn't.

Heath eyed the time on his rose gold Patek Philippe. Alicia had walked away over forty-five minutes ago. He'd seen her grandmother rejoin the party at least thirty minutes earlier. What the fuck was taking his betrothed so damn long? She should've returned by fucking now. He dipped his chin at his companions. "Excuse me." Victor had sworn to him she understood her role as his fiancée. If this was something he could expect, then he'd need to train her better.

Scanning the crowd, he scrutinized the various partygoers. While he didn't recognize everyone who joined the celebration, he knew most of the faces. No one appeared out of place. They'd all dressed appropriately for the occasion. All conversed with someone he'd already met or knew firsthand. No party crashers. Nothing out of the ordinary.

There had to be some other explanation then for her unexpected disappearance. He spotted Alicia's older sister first. She might not know a damn thing, but she still seemed like a good place to start. And she'd be less likely to hold back any truths from him. Heath strode across the parlor, listening to the conversations as he passed by other patrons. Nothing really caught his attention, except perhaps one conversation. A couple of those gathered discussed shifts in the supernatural world, but didn't go into details.

If it affected the witches, their priestess would have requested they dig into it. That certainly hadn't happened. Bad news always traveled faster than good. Heath quickly dismissed it and focused on his goal. He stopped next to Angel and her husband, Nicholas. Shoving his hands into the pockets of his slacks, Heath flashed a pearly white smile. "I don't suppose either of you have seen my better half?"

Angel tilted her head and pursed her lips. "No. I thought she was with you."

This female couldn't be that ignorant. If Alicia had been by his side, he wouldn't have fucking asked, would he? Good Lilith, what the fuck had his parents agreed to by joining with the Cromwell faction? "What about your father? Perhaps I should speak with him."

"There." Nicholas gestured toward a side door. One that he suspected led to the kitchen.

"Appreciated." At least one of them had proven useful. Though the way Angel wrung her hands bothered him. Did she know something and simply refused to share it? Had she actually seen Alicia? A conversation with Victor would help. The male could get his daughters under control. Heath turned and headed in the guy's direction.

Victor's eyebrows furrowed as he approached. The male frowned. "Heath, where's Alicia?"

His eyes narrowed at the confusion written clear as day on the male's face. If everything had gone according to plan, then he'd know exactly where his wife-to-be was. At all times. Obviously, that hadn't happened. Heath smirked. "That's what I'd like to know. She went upstairs some time ago and never returned."

Blinking rapidly, Victor blanched. "What? I'm sure you're mistaken, and she's here somewhere."

Had the male just called him a liar? Surely that wasn't the case. Glowering at Victor, Heath stepped closer. Although he hadn't yet uttered a single word, the way the male's eyes widened confirmed the male received the message. "I'm going to give you the benefit of the doubt here. But I suggest you find Alicia quickly and quietly. I'll not have her embarrass me, especially at our engagement party."

Victor visibly swallowed. "Don't worry. I'll find her and get her back to your side."

"Good." Adding fuel to the fire, Heath squeezed the male's shoulder tightly. "And remind her of her duties to me. Training her isn't on my agenda. If I have to do it, then it won't be pleasant for all parties involved."

"Understood."

That was exactly what he wanted to hear. Heath released the hold he had on Victor and grinned as the male scurried off. With that handled, Heath tugged the cuffs of his shirt back in place and rejoined the party. It was a celebration. One he intended to fully enjoy.

Lewis grumbled under his breath as he stole a sidelong glance at the blonde beside him. Her incessant questions weren't the only thing that irritated the fuck out of him. She was a fucking witch. Of all the creatures Holloway could've directed him toward, what the fuck convinced the cat a witch could help? A witch had gotten him into this mess. Like he'd trust another to get him out of it. The sound of crunching leaves tickled his ears.

"Answer me—"

Cutting her off, he covered her mouth, spun them around, and pressed tight against a nearby tree trunk. It was large enough to hide them from whatever came their way. The tunnel entrance wasn't too much farther, but he couldn't risk its discovery. He'd stayed safe all these years by remaining well-hidden and keeping off the Red Queen's radar. One round with that bitch was enough for him. A pretty blonde witch wouldn't fuck that up now.

Her aroma wafted in the air, titillating his nostrils. Gods, she smelled like a combination of spice and wood. Despite the shivers that shot down his spine, he kept his composure. Pressing harder against the tree, the trunk's bark bit into his back. The slight sting helped him focus. Lewis listened to the hoard of shuffling feet. It had to be the Red Queen's guards.

Were they searching for him?

Or her?

Either option made sense. Not that he'd let them get anywhere near the female in his arms. Fuck, she felt damn good pressed against him like this. He couldn't recall the last time he'd stood this close to a woman. Something he shouldn't even be thinking about right then. They were close to being discovered by the Red Queen's soldiers. He needed to focus on that shit.

What the fuck was this woman doing to him? Releasing his hand from her narrow waist, Lewis tilted his head as a few soldiers shuffled right by where they hid. The men halted. The little witch stiffened against him. At least it seemed she finally understood the gravity of the threat that chased them.

"Are you sure they went this way? There's nothing but a bunch of trees."

"Maybe they backtracked."

"Or they've already left the forest, and you didn't see shit."

"Shut up! I know what I saw."

Lewis frowned. He heard a slight chuff echo around them. It sounded like one person slapping another. Great. If they kept this up, then waiting them out might not be their best choice.

"Knock it off! Both of you!" one male hollered. "We need to find them. Now. So, we split up."

"Yes, sir," the other two stated simultaneously.

Three sets of feet jogged off in separate directions. The blonde glanced at him. He shook his head and pressed a finger against his lips. They had to give them a couple of minutes to get far enough away before they moved.

She dipped her chin, acknowledging his response. Her sapphire-blue eyes left his face and scanned their surroundings.

His gaze dropped to the gentle curve of her features. Her honey-blonde locks fanned her cheeks, framing the long line of her neck, and hung past her shoulders. Lewis balled up his fists, digging his nails into his palms. It didn't stop the urge to reach out and touch her, but at least it stopped him from acting on it. Her ample lips pinched together.

He looked away before he did something he'd regret. So what if she had an hourglass figure that called out to the depths of his desires? Or an exquisite pair of blue eyes that twinkled under the moonlight? Or a gaze that seemed to peer into the recesses of his soul? None of that mattered.

Because no fucking way would he ever have a damn thing to do with another witch. It was bad enough he risked his life helping her. That didn't mean he had to learn a single thing about her. Not even her fucking name.

Facing him, she cocked a refined eyebrow at him. She gestured toward the lush shrubbery. Yeah. They'd stood here long enough. Or so he hoped. Brushing past her, he pushed forward and strode deeper into the forest.

"Can you warn me next time?" she whispered harshly.

"Excuse me?" Hadn't she figured out the soldiers were after them? Or had she already forgotten what chased after her?

"Before you grab me again. A warning would be great."

Lewis scoffed. Was she fucking with him? He glimpsed at her. Something shone in those opalescent-blue eyes of hers, but he couldn't quite make it out. Instead of answering, he continued on and closed the short distance between them and the tunnel entrance. He paused at a crosshatch covered by a pile of leaves.

"Why are we stopping?"

"We're here." Lifting the camouflaged entrance, he pointed to the open hole in the ground.

"Do you expect me to go down there?"

"Your choice, princess." He shrugged. It didn't bother him one way or the other. That was a bald-faced lie. He had this unexplainable desire to keep her close to his side. His jaw clenched, and he rolled his shoulders. Though it hardly helped ease the tension in his body. His gaze flicked from her to the hole and back again. Waiting around for her to decide didn't do either of them any good. "Do what you want, but I'm going down and getting the fuck out of the Whispering Woods!"

Without another word, Lewis propped up the cover and placed his foot on the closest rung. She had until he reached the bottom of the ladder to decide. He'd close the top from down there, protecting the tunnel entrance.

At all costs.

Or so he tried to convince himself.

CHAPTER
Three

CARTER TAPPED HER long fingernails against her throne's arm. She glowered at the three idiots that stood before her. Yeah, they fucking hung their heads in shame, but that only irritated her further. "How the fuck could you lose them?!"

"My apologies, Your Majesty. I should've taken better control of the situation."

She rose from her seat and descended the staircase, purposely avoiding the red rug that ran from the throne down the center. Her high heels clicked against the marble floor with each step she took, echoing around the throne room. The train of her red-chiffon dress trailed behind her. As did her knave. He never lingered too far from her presence. "Yes, you should have, Lieutenant. Your apology means shit to me. What do you plan to do to fix it?" Something had to be done. She couldn't allow her subjects to help strangers that randomly arrived in their land. Especially not one that could ruin everything she'd built.

The dark-haired male visibly swallowed. His gaze locked on the floor. "With your permission, we will go to the city on the morrow, roust any spellcasters, and set them ablaze."

"That's a start." She watched as their shoulders sagged in relief. Did they think this meant she'd forgiven them? No. Nor did it give them a reprieve. Carter summoned a blood-red sword to her hand and, in one swift move, she swung it in an arc and sliced through the closest soldier's neck. The male's head slid to the ground with a slight thud. Crimson liquid splattered everywhere. A few droplets landed on the deep V-neck of her dress. "Be sure you cause a loud ruckus." Her gaze flicked to one of her handmaidens. "Clean this up."

Disappearing the blade, she sashayed across the throne room and left. They could wallow in their misery for all she cared. No one would forget this lesson. Nothing like this would happen again. Not on her watch.

"Was that really necessary, Your Majesty?" Jaq asked as he followed her.

"They should be grateful I made his death so quick." She glanced at her second-in-command. "And that I didn't add more to the pile." Because she'd considered it. It was also something she'd done in the past, but what the male presented her warranted leniency. She gave them that.

"Very well." He interlocked his fingers at the small of his back as they entered the lengthy hallway. "Are you positive this book is our means of escape?"

"Oh, absolutely. We just need to play everything perfectly, which means you have your mission while those idiots have theirs." Carter lifted the thick, leather-bound book and inhaled deeply. How she missed that sweet, woodsy scent. Centuries had passed since the last time she'd seen this tome. "We've searched for this witch for a long time. You cannot screw this up. Do you understand?"

"I'm well aware of the importance of our actions. That's why you mustn't allow your greed to get the better of you." He narrowed his dark-brown eyes at her.

Halting in her steps, she disappeared the Cromwell grimoire and shoved him against the wall. Carter closed the short distance between them, wrapped a hand around his throat, and tightened her grip. "Don't forget who is in charge. You may have found the book, but you only stumbled on it. I'm the one who got us here."

"And got us trapped to begin with," he snapped. "Or have you forgotten that?"

Of course, she hadn't. Those miserable witches hadn't recognized the depth of their curse. Or how far she'd go to break it. Letting up a touch, she pressed her body flush against his, licked his cheek, and nipped his ear. "Then maybe we should celebrate. Because we're finally getting the fuck out of here." Between the two of them, they'd play that little witch like a fiddle and lead her exactly where they wanted her to be.

"I'm all for a celebration." He grabbed her arms, spun her around, and slammed her against the wall. With the hit, the stone bit into her shoulder blades. The sting sent a blaze of heat straight to her core. Placing his hands on either side of her, Jaq pinned her in. The hard planes of his chest pressed against her tits, hardening her nipples. He fused his lips to hers, entangling their tongues.

She moaned into the kiss. *Fuck, yes.* His hands slid down her back and gripped her ass. As he lifted her off the ground, her legs automatically wrapped around his waist. They should take this into her room, but she was far too eager to wait. It wasn't as if anyone saw them. The hallway remained empty save for the two of them.

Jaq ground his rigid shaft against her pussy. Even with the layers of clothing between them, she felt the thickness of his erection. He bit her tongue, drawing a groan out of her. Fuck, yes, she liked it when he got rough with her. Gripping the top of his vest, she ripped it straight down the middle and raked her nails down his back. Blood beaded beneath the thin fabric of his tunic. It wasn't enough. She needed to feel his flesh under her fingertips.

A low rumble resounded in his chest. His claws tore through the layers of her dress as he buried them in her ass cheek and dragged the claws on his other hand across the supple flesh of her shoulder blades. The burn sent blasts of heat straight to her core. Fuck, she was already so wet. How much more would he torture her before he fucked her raw?

Biting her tongue, he broke off the kiss. "A little eager, are we? Tell me, Your Majesty, do you want me to fuck you right here and now? In the hall? Visible to all?"

"Yes," she purred. That was what she wanted. She needed to feel his cock throbbing deep inside of her. Emphasizing her answer, Carter tightened her grip on his waist, rocked her hips, and pressed her pussy more against the bulge in his pants.

"Then beg me," Jaq drawled. She felt his warm breath on her neck as he skimmed his fangs along her throat. The strip of fabric across her shoulders loosened. Part of her dress slid down her arms as the front fell forward, bunching up between them and freeing her breasts.

Fuck. This dragon knew how to drive her crazy. Begging for anything wasn't her style. That included getting him to fuck her. Especially when they both knew he wanted it just as badly as she did. She simply needed to remind him who was in charge. Carter glided her long fingers underneath his tunic and dug them into his taut back. His scales shimmered beneath her palm. "I'm your Queen. You do as I say. If I want you to fuck me, then you'll fuck me. If I want you to take me into the throne room and fuck my pussy with your tongue, you'll do it. Understood?"

"Well, you *are* my Queen," he retorted. "That is a fact." His deft fingers threaded through her dark locks. Jaq fisted a handful of her hair and jerked her head back. "But you're not in charge right now," he growled. "*I* am. You'll do as *I* say. Got it?"

Carter barely bit back a groan. He didn't need her noises to stroke his ego. Something this man had in spades. That didn't mean she wouldn't answer him or follow his command. They'd played this game before. And Jaq always won. "Yes, Sir."

"Good girl." Shoving a knee under her ass, he adjusted his hold. His hand slid under the satin and chiffon material of her dress. He skimmed his claws across her inner thigh, inching closer to that junction between her legs. "Now, beg me, my little queen."

Fuck, she both hated and loved when he got like this. She'd do anything to get him where they both desired. Even beg. "Fuck me, hard, please, Sir. Against the wall. Please, Sir. Like everyone is waiting, watching, and you're their instructor. Please… *Sir.*" Carter bit his ear, tugging on it. "Fuck me like I need a punishment. Please, Sir."

"Is that all you want, little queen? Or do you want something more?" His thumb stroked her slit through the thin cotton of her panties.

A soft gasp left her mouth as a blast of heat speared right through her. Her back arched, pressing her pussy more against him. She didn't think his torture could get worse. Had it been so long since their last time together she forgot all the agonizing ways he liked to tease the fuck out of her? "I want all of it. Every touch, grip… your claws… pain… All. Of. It."

Jaq yanked her head back, drawing a moan out of her. "What did you forget?"

Shit. Two words she loathed more than anything. But she needed him with more desperation than she experienced before. "Please, Sir. Fuck me with your fingers. Make me bleed with your claws. Torment me… please… like only you can, Sir."

"Mmm. That's what I like to hear." His hand slipped beneath her panties and his fingers delved into the moist, warm folds between her thighs, making her buck forward. As he drove his digits deeper into her pussy, he skated his tongue along her breast and took her nipple between his teeth.

"Fuck!" Carter cried out. Jaq didn't ease into anything. Not that she wanted easy. Fire burned hot inside of her, demanding, rough, as if tomorrow didn't exist for them. The two fingers he pumped in and out of her stoked the blaze, lighting up her synapses. She slid her hand up his sculpted back and dug her heels into his ass cheeks.

A deep rumble resounded in his chest. He circled the tip of his tongue around her hardened nipple and skimmed his fangs across her breast. "So wet for me, but I think we can do better." Adding a third finger to the mix, Jaq increased his pace and penetrated her pussy faster and harder.

Holy shit, he was trying to stretch her out. As if she required the preparation for his girth. Each stroke of his fingers sent a jolt of electricity straight to her core. She swung her hips, riding his digits, heightening the sensations ripping through her body. Heat pooled between her thighs. Although she held the release back, it achingly sat on the edge. "May I come, please, Sir?"

"No." Letting loose a guttural growl, he raked his claws across the soft skin of her inner thigh.

The fire raging in her lower belly intensified. Her slick folds clamped his fingers, pulsating with a feverish heat. It took every ounce of control she had to stop the orgasm, demanding its freedom. *Fuck.* She desperately needed his rigid length to fill her up. Begging got them nowhere. Perhaps, if she pushed him to the brink. Carter dragged her hand over the bare skin of his waist, dropped her hand between them, and skated her fingertips across the bulge in his leather pants.

"I didn't give you permission to touch," he grunted. His fingers stilled inside of her.

"But you didn't say I couldn't, either… *Sir,*" Carter purred. Her hand wrapped around the hardness of his arousal, squeezing it. She knew what buttons of his to push. At this rate, he'd snap and inflict glorious pain on her body.

Withdrawing his fingers from her pussy, Jaq grabbed her wrist and jerked it from his shaft. "That doesn't mean you can do what you desire, little queen. You follow *my* rules. Do what I let you. It seems you need a reminder of what happens when you don't listen." He pulled her legs from around his waist and spun her around so she faced the wall. Taking her wrists in his hand, he pinned her arms above her head. "Don't fucking move," he snarled.

Biting back a moan, Carter clenched her thighs and held her impending orgasm at bay. Fuck. Every synapse in her body lit up like a full moon. His rough manhandling turned the heat in the deep recesses of her core into a volcano on the verge of explosion. She wouldn't dream of moving. Not yet.

He gripped the top of her dress's skirting and ripped it right down the middle. It fell away from her body, pooling in a pile at her feet. Her underwear quickly followed. Jaq anchored his hands around her narrow waist and cocked her hips, popping her ass out. "No matter what happens, little queen, don't you fucking come." He smoothed a hand over her backside as his palm connected with her other cheek.

"Fuck," she groaned. Shit. She pushed his buttons. All the right ones, too. Though perhaps a bit too much. While she yearned to have him punish her, withholding an orgasm wasn't at the top of her ideal list of punishments.

Cupping her ass, he squeezed and massaged her backside and drew his hand back. His calloused palm landed against her soft flesh three more times with a loud slap. "Such a good girl." Jaq threaded his fingers into her silky tresses as he leaned over her. "Tell me, little queen…" His words trailed off. He skimmed his fangs across her satin-smooth shoulder. "How badly do you need me to fuck you right now?"

Her need was perilous. The way her ass stung from the spanking sent waves of immense pleasure ripping through her body. A massive orgasm teetered so close to the fringe. She didn't know how much longer she could hold back. "Please, please, please fuck me hard, Sir." Glancing at him, Carter pushed her ass back against him. Begging and showing him how much she needed his cock.

"As you wish." He undid his buckle, yanked his leather pants apart, buttons flying everywhere, and his erection sprang forth. As Jaq sank his fangs into her shoulder, he pressed the head of his shaft against her entrance and slammed into her.

Carter cried out in pure ecstasy. Her fingernails scraped the wall as she clung to her release. It threatened to erupt out of her. She didn't give a shit that he hadn't given her permission. That mattered little in the grand scheme of things. The longer she held back, the more powerful it would be. Though she was ready for it. She rocked her hips back against his cock. Her cunt squeezed his shaft. Each stroke of his rigid length sent pleasure pulsating through her.

Jerking his teeth from her shoulder, Jaq growled. Curling his fingers around her slim waist, he dug his claws into the rounded curve of her hip.

Blood trickled down her flesh. Wasting no time to build a steady rhythm, he pounded into her.

The harder and faster his strokes came, the more his balls slapped against her ass. Fuck. She couldn't hold back any longer. "Please, please, please let me come, Sir. Please!"

"Fuck! Come for me!"

They both screamed at the high that ignited between them. Jaq pummeled her slick folds as her pussy tightened around his thickness. A potent orgasm detonated deep inside of her and drenched his shaft. His roar bounced off the walls as a release gushed out of him, spilling down the back of her thighs. Neither of them stilled until they'd worked through their mutual orgasm. His hand came around and gripped her breast, kneading it. He rolled her nipple between his thumb and forefinger. "Don't think we're finished," Jaq rasped. "I'm nowhere near done with you."

The corners of her mouth curled into a smile as she glanced at him over her shoulder. "Good. Because I'm not finished, either." They were just getting started. When they were both spent, they could take care of business and set their prey on a path, years in the making.

Nothing could stop them from getting the freedom they deserved. Everything they wanted and more was finally within their grasps. And they'd get it. No matter who they had to kill.

Alicia eyed the ladder leading into a tunnel. The sound of leaves crunching tickled her ears. She flicked her gaze toward the noise. Shit. Did she take a chance with the soldiers and whatever beast chased after her? Or follow some ruggedly handsome stranger down the rabbit hole? "Fuck," she muttered. It didn't seem she had any other choice. *Goddess, don't let me regret this.* Taking a step forward, she turned around and eased a high-heeled foot onto the closest rung.

"Today, princess!" the male hollered.

Slowly, she descended the ladder. One spoke at a time. *Arrogant, impatient asshole.* Like he could climb down this damn thing with stilettos. She was lucky she hadn't tripped the whole time she ran through the woods. Or that a root hadn't caught—missing the next step. Her foot slipped out from under her. Alicia fell backward, landing on top of him and knocking him to the dirt floor.

They both grunted.

"Shit. Sorry." Twisting her body slightly, she pressed her hands against the hard planes of his abs. Alicia swallowed, fighting back the heat that speared through her, as she quickly scrambled to her feet. She hadn't meant to touch him, but her limbs had a mind of their own.

"Shut up," he whispered harshly. He leaped to his feet and yanked on a nearby lever. The opening above them closed, shrouding them both in darkness.

Before she opened her mouth, his hand came over it. He seriously needed to fucking stop that. At least he hadn't stood behind her this time. She didn't need to feel any part of his body pressed against hers. The last time she'd stood there noticing every hard angle and muscle beneath his dirty white tunic. Her eyes lifted toward the ceiling at the sound of muffled voices above them.

Not that she could discern anything. They sounded so far off, yet so close at the same time. She didn't know how long they stayed in that one spot. Her gaze shifted in the male's direction. At least the direction she imagined he stood, given his hand over her mouth and the heat pouring off of him.

"They're gone," he mumbled, removing his hand. "We should be good to go."

"How are we supposed to do that? You got a flashlight… or… torch?" The latter made more sense. She saw nothing denoting a time period. Except his attire and that of the soldiers. If she hazarded a guess, she'd think somewhere around the 1600s. Which made no sense whatsoever. Then again, her grandmother said someone enchanted the egg centuries ago. Maybe that was when the egg had been created. None of which mattered right then. They needed to see where they walked.

"Right," the male snorted and shuffled around. "Give me your hand."

"Why? So, the blind can lead the blind?" Alicia scoffed. Like that would resolve their problem. Besides, she didn't entirely trust him. For fuck's sake, she didn't even know his name!

He captured her hand in his, stroking her palm with his thumb, and pressed something small, wet, and spongy in her hand. "Here. Eat this. It'll help."

"What is it?" Shivers shot down her spine. Frowning, she curled her fingers around it and lifted it to her nose. It had an umbrella shape to it. She gave it a small sniff. The sweet aroma of cinnamon and vanilla wafted into her nostrils. Was it a mushroom?

"Do you always ask so many questions? Just fucking eat it."

"When I'm somewhere I don't know shit about, yes. It isn't like you've been forthcoming about where I ended up. You could be trying to poison me for all I know." Maybe if he answered any of her questions, she wouldn't irritate him so much. With every attempt she made along their trek through the forest, he silenced her.

"You're in a secret passageway that leads us out of the Whispering Woods," he snapped. "Now, eat."

It wasn't much, but it was better than nothing. "Fine," Alicia grumbled, tossed the tiny piece of food into her mouth, and chewed it. Noting the texture, it was definitely a mushroom with an earthy flavor to it. She swallowed it. What was it supposed to—? "Whoa." She blinked and stared at the lustrous glow lining the uneven walls. It lit the whole cavern up.

"There. Problem solved. Now, let's go." The male spun on the back of his heel and started forward.

Why the fuck did he keep doing that? Was he determined to leave her behind? Alicia darted after him. "Where are we going exactly? Besides, away from the Whispering Woods? Because I don't know where that is. I don't know where I am, period."

"You're in Wonder, princess. Ruled by the Red Queen. Those were her men after us. Anything else you want to know? Or can we actually make this trip in silence?"

Bad things happened when stillness surrounded her. Yeah, she cared little for the quiet. Except when she researched. That was impossible right now. "How about your name?" She needed something. His name was a small ask.

Halting in his steps, he dragged a hand through his thick, brown hair and faced her. His lips pressed into a thin line. As his jaw set, he leaned in close. "One condition. We make the rest of this trip in complete silence. You don't ask me anything or tell me anything. I don't need to know a damn thing about you. Deal?"

Alicia took in a sharp breath. Heat flooded her cheeks. She averted her gaze from those golden-brown orbs of his. There was something about the way he looked at her. It was almost like he wanted to eat her up or strangle her. Perhaps both. Her eyes locked on his. For a split second, she swore his eyes darkened. At that moment, she'd do whatever he desired. "Agreed."

He visibly swallowed and cleared his throat. "Um, Lewis. My name is Lewis. Now, uh, let's move."

Although she loathed the idea of silence, she'd follow through. As long as he got her somewhere safe. That was all that mattered. The rest, she could figure out later. Or so she hoped.

CHAPTER
four

"WHERE IS SHE, Angel?" Heath glowered at the blonde-haired female as he followed her up the staircase. Nearly thirty minutes had passed since he had spoken with Angel and her father. Now Victor summoned him like some commoner? Who the fuck did this male think he was? They'd either located his betrothed or they hadn't. Simple enough. This whole parlor show, with the long walk up to the guy's study, wasn't necessary.

"You should really discuss this with my father," she replied over her shoulder without looking at him.

That didn't bode well for the situation. Which meant one thing and one thing only. That bitch left; pulled some kind of disappearing act. At their engagement party. She'd pay for embarrassing him like this. As would Victor. Not that he knew how yet, but he'd figure it out.

They rounded the second-floor landing, turned right, and headed down the hallway. Gripping the doorknob, Angel rapped on the door and eased it open. "Father. He's here."

"Show him in," Victor said.

The female stepped aside, giving him berth to enter the lavish study. Heath strode past her. Normally, he took a moment and investigated his surroundings, but that was the least of his concerns. He only cared about answers. The male had better give him every single one that he desired.

Victor waved the female off. "Return to the party, Angel. We'll rejoin you shortly."

"Yes, Father." She bowed her head and departed, closing the door behind her.

At least one of the male's daughters knew how to act. Too bad it wasn't his betrothed. It would've made the evening go much differently. His green eyes settled on Alicia's father as the heavy oak door clicked shut. Heath folded his arms across his chest. "Where is she, Victor?"

"Missing." A heavy sigh escaped the male. "It seems she left the house not long after she spoke with her grandmother."

Heath flexed his fingers and ground his teeth at the rage that boiled just beneath the surface. He expected more than the obvious. The male knew better than to string him along. Narrowing his gaze, he closed the distance between them and an executive desk. "Tell me something I haven't ascertained for myself," he snapped. "Where the fuck is she, Victor? Because right now, the only conclusion I can draw is that you've lied about everything regarding Alicia. So, don't give me some bullshit line, hoping to placate me. I want actual answers." He slammed his fist down on the oak furniture. "Understood?"

Jumping up, Victor knocked the chair over as he surged forward, slapped his hand on the desk's surface, and jabbed a finger in Heath's face. "I don't give a shit who you are. It'll do you good to remember whose house you're in!"

He refused to apologize for his actions. The male owed him one hell of an explanation. "Then I suggest you get straight with me. Because all I have are a lot of assumptions. Is your daughter even as powerful as you claimed? As obedient? Or have you sold me a false set of goods?"

A haggard expression settled across the male's features as his lips pinched into a white slash. "Alicia is special. Unique. Her powers are unlike anyone else in our family."

"That sounds like a load of bullshit." Nothing more than a fancy line people used when they had no genuine answer. "I suggest you try again," Heath growled.

Victor dragged a hand through his short, blond hair and blew out a heavy breath. "Until she binds herself to her other half, her spells can fizzle quickly. Once she is bound, our entire line will feel the true magnitude of her power."

One simple truth and his entire mood soured. How the fuck was he supposed to react to this news? Folding his arms across his pecs, Heath crossed the room and stopped in front of a bookcase. He inhaled and exhaled a shallow breath as he eyed the various trinkets. Not that he really paid any of them any mind. It just kept him from setting the male on fire. Despite the urge to do so. He glowered at Victor. "So, basically, her power is useless until the bonding ceremony?"

"Alicia isn't useless," he retorted. "Her spells may not carry the same weight as the rest of us, but it doesn't make her less than."

"'The same weight?' That's your answer?" Heath sneered. Had the male lost his fucking mind? Did the guy think those three words meant something different to their factions? Because they didn't. "She is either up to my standard or you sold me a subpar set of goods. Which is it?"

"I did no such thing! When we started negotiations, I told you her power hadn't yet fully manifested, but we have incredible expectations from her. Alicia is the future of our bloodline. She will carry our faction forward. I wouldn't have promised her to you if I believed anything less than that."

"Fair enough." But he required more than the male's word that her power matched his abilities. They would test every theory presented… once they found her. This still left one thing unaddressed. "And her insolence?"

"Alicia is the perfect match for you, Heath. Her mother is aware of the situation and will rectify any training… issues… that you've identified. We'll have them resolved before your—"

"No," Heath cut him off. Any chance for them to resolve the problem had passed. He had expectations, as did his family. They had measures in place when something like this occurred. "Your wife will do nothing, nor will you. I'll handle her reconditioning." Given the circumstances, it was necessary. His faction held stronger connections in the community and more authority than the Cromwell family. His betrothed needed to measure up to all of it. It made him better suited to resolve her training missteps.

"Heath, I assure you, that's unnecessary. We're capable—"

"Of finding her. Nothing more. Once you have and I'm confident Alicia *is* the best match for me, we'll proceed with the nuptials as planned." Facing Victor, Heath met the male's gaze and steepled his fingers together in front of him. If he needed to remind the man in another way of his position, then he'd do just that. It wouldn't take more than a look. It rarely did. "Are we clear?"

"Perfectly."

"Good. I'm glad we had this discussion." The last few minutes gave him more insight into Alicia's personality than he'd gotten all evening. It better prepared him for the battles that lay ahead. Because one thing was definitely clear—this wasn't the end of them.

Lewis turned the knob and gave the door a gentle nudge. It swung open with a slight creak. He gestured for the blonde witch to go first. The place remained as empty as he'd left it and just as minimally furnished. Despite all his years in Wonder, he required little.

Leaning around him, she peered into his humble abode and hesitantly took a step forward. She cocked an eyebrow at him. "You don't lock your door? That doesn't seem safe. What if someone snuck in while you were away? Or stole something?"

No one had ever found his sanctuary, accidentally or otherwise. If they happened upon it, they hadn't entered it and there wasn't much for them to steal. Animals pretty much let him be. Instead of a verbal response, he half grunted as he followed her and shut the door.

"Where are we exactly?"

"Home." It was the simplest of answers, but he didn't want to encourage conversation. They'd made the trip here in blessed silence. That took a lot of effort on his part. It irritated him how much he longed to hear her voice. He'd never heard something so soothing and melodic. *Damn witch.* Lewis strode across the room, stopping in front of the stone fireplace. Ash and blackened wood chunks filled it. He kneeled down to sweep it out some.

"I'm sorry? Your home? You brought me to your place? Have you lost your fucking mind? I don't know a damn thing about you. Why would you bring me here?"

He stole a side-long glimpse at her. The hairs on the nape of his neck stood at attention. His heartbeat quickened. Just a look and this female stole his breath. What the fuck was she doing to him? Shaking the sensations from his body, he stacked a few logs onto the metal grate. "It's the safest place for you, princess."

"Alicia!" she yelled. "My name is Alicia. Not princess or sweetheart or whatever other asinine pet name you can come up with."

Alicia. Lewis rolled her name around in his head. If he uttered it aloud, he'd give far too much away. Even if he did, he refused to do a damn thing about his attraction to her. No witch would get to him. Not again. "Whatever."

"Thank you for getting me out of the woods, but I require no more of your assistance. I'll be safer on my own." She headed for the exit.

Lewis glanced over his shoulder. Surely, she'd die if he let her walk out the front door. What if what Holloway said was true? And this woman *was* his way out? No way could he allow her to leave. He hopped to his feet, jumped in front of her, and closed the distance between them. "You don't know shit about Wonder, princess. I promise you won't be safe. A witch like you… they'll burn alive. That's only if the other creatures don't sink their fangs into you first."

Her blue eyes widened. She slowly backed away until he pinned her against the couch. "How… how do you know… about me?"

A smirk played on the corners of his mouth as he placed a hand on either side of her. "Because I know how to recognize *your* kind," he spat out. "But if you think you can survive out there, by all means, take your best shot."

"How do I know I'm any safer in here with you than out there being hunted?"

"You don't. Except I haven't tried to kill you." Did he seriously have to remind her that he'd saved her? Twice. Maybe he didn't trust her, but at least he had that going for him.

Alicia tilted her head and narrowed her gaze at him, as if she sized him up. Silence stretched between them for a beat. "Right, but I don't suspect that was out of the goodness of your heart. You need me, don't you? I'm not the only one who's trapped, am I?"

One hell of a conclusion to draw. Yeah, it was fucking accurate, but he hadn't given shit away. Not that it mattered. Lewis leaned in close. Her rich, woodsy scent thickened, filling his nostrils. *Oh, gods.* She smelled fucking fantastic. His muscles tensed as a blast of unadulterated lust shot through him. He rolled his shoulders. Though it did little to ease the friction that his body generated, he refused to act on his desires. It was a likely result of his lack of romantic endeavors than a genuine attraction to this witch. "Regardless of why, I'm the only protection you've got."

Drawing herself up to her full height, she lifted her chin and met his gaze. "I can protect myself." She closed what little space remained between them and balled up her fists.

A violent gust of wind knocked him back. Although he stayed on his feet, he stumbled backward a few steps.

"Like you said… I'm a witch. Don't you forget it." Smirking, Alicia stormed off down the hallway, entered his bedroom, and slammed the door shut behind her.

Lewis stared after her. Her little act of defiance left him with a raging hard-on. He strode forward, stopping halfway to his bedroom, and shoved a hand through his hair. What the fuck was he thinking? Fuck. This damn witch was going to be the death of him. Maybe it was a good thing she disappeared into his bedroom. Neither of them needed him to act on the instincts roaring through him right now.

Turning around, he took a couple of steps forward and halted. He glanced at his bedroom door and sniffed the air. Her scent shouldn't have lingered like this… unless… had she gotten… aroused? No. Impossible. Except… He scrubbed a hand across his face. It didn't matter. Alicia was a witch and he was a shifter. Their kind didn't mix. For a good reason. Even if they did, no way would he ever trust another witch. Not even Alicia.

He only needed her for one thing—to escape Wonder. Once they'd done that, they'd go their separate ways. Lewis rubbed at the ache setting up shop in his heart. It was the only way this worked. Because he'd never give himself over to another witch. Not again.

Jaq drummed his fingers against his arm as Carter chanted and sliced a silver blade across her palm. Blood welled in her hand as she lifted it in the air and spilled it all over the human heart out on display. The gusts of wind and flickering lights reassured him of the spell she cast. It was good to know he hadn't sacrificed a chambermaid for nothing. Provided everything else went according to their plan.

Tilting his head, he flicked his tongue across a fang as the speed of the wind intensified. The metallic aroma of her blood wafted all around him. It took every ounce of self-control he mustered not to go over there, tear that black and crimson dress of hers to shreds, and fuck her all over again. As soon as she finished the incantation, all bets were off. He had plenty of time to set everything in motion.

As the last word left Carter's mouth, the bare walls shook and the empty wooden floors vibrated. A flash of red light pulsated through the bloody heart, rippling out of the room in a steady current. "What the fuck?" Jaq snarled. "I thought you said no one would realize what we'd done."

Her dark gaze snapped in his direction. "Then you didn't listen. I said no one except true kin of mine would notice the spell."

He stalked across the room and grabbed her arm, leaving an imprint of his fingers in her flesh. "That isn't what I fucking agreed to."

"We can't take it back now, can we? It's all in motion. So, I suggest you fucking suck it up and do what you have to do."

Suck it up? It appeared she needed another lesson regarding her attitude. Jaq wrapped a hand around her neck, gripped tight, and gently stroked his talon across her throat. He pressed his face close to hers. "You're lucky I want to get the fuck out of here. While I should punish you here and now for your lack of clarity, I've got a better idea."

Carter visibly swallowed. "Oh?"

Her arousal practically saturated the air. It was so fucking thick; he could almost taste it. He flicked his tongue across her flesh and leaned closer to her ear. "I'm going to run these errands… quickly. When I return, you should be naked except for the ruby-studded collar and in a present position." Although he'd enjoyed tearing her dress to shreds earlier, and he longed to do it again, he'd rather mar that beautiful, creamy-white skin of hers instead. It would look glorious, painted in a pattern of blues, purples, and crimson.

"Yes, Sir," she purred.

"Good girl." Releasing her throat, he stepped back ever so slightly and held out his hand. "Now give me the grimoire and athame." Before they played, he had work to do.

Alicia inhaled and exhaled a deep breath. What the hell just transpired between them? How had he gotten to her so easily? No one had ever gotten under her skin the way this male did. Not even her so-called betrothed. From her position on the bed, she eyed the room and checked out its lack of décor.

Nothing covered the walls. Not a painting of any kind. Nothing lay across the hardwood floor. No rug. Nothing. The comforter and pillows placed on the bed were simple. Just a plain dark blue. At least it matched the same as the living room. She paid little attention to everything else, including the kitchen.

The surrounding air pulsated with an undulating light, which was strange. It only ever happened when… impossible. Jumping to her feet, she darted across the room and yanked the door open. Alicia halted as she spotted Lewis kneeled by the fireplace, stacking logs into it. Nothing appeared out of the ordinary.

This made little sense. Her eyebrows squished together as she rubbed her forehead. She swore she saw the ripple effect of blood magic. Something that only a member of her family could've properly conducted. Yes, other witches used similar spells, but if that was the case, she wouldn't have detected it.

Lewis peered over his shoulder at her and returned his attention back to the fire, stoking the flames. "Did you think of something else you needed to say? Or have you come to apologize?"

"Me? Apologize?" Alicia retorted. She folded her arms across her chest and glowered at him. "What the fuck do I have to apologize for? You're the one that made several assumptions." Although most of them were entirely inaccurate, at least one was right. Not that she wanted to verbalize it.

"Throwing me across the room. That would be a good start. Followed by storming off amidst a conversation."

She bit back a smirk. While she'd give him the second, the first was utter bullshit. "One, I didn't throw you. Just gave you a slight nudge." They'd gotten far too close to one another and she'd liked it way too much. "Two…" She half-shrugged. "Obviously, we need to come to some sort of… agreement. A way for us to work together." They required one another. She didn't know what surprises awaited her out there and her magic was often unpredictable. She couldn't guarantee a repeat of what had happened earlier.

Setting the metal poker aside, he rose to his feet. "And you have a proposition?"

"Yes, but before I share my thoughts, I need you to answer something." More than what little he'd already shared. That hadn't given her anything to go on.

"You can ask, but I won't promise an answer. Or at least one you'll like."

Yeah. She expected that much. Though she hoped he actually gave her something genuine. And that she could hold up her end of the bargain. "Tell me how you ended up here. You answer that and I think we can make a deal. One that benefits us both."

CHAPTER
five

AS JAQ APPROACHED the corridor to the queen's quarters, he scrutinized the soldier stationed outside the hall. The male stood there, stoic and unresponsive. Just as he'd trained all of his men to do. No noise should startle the man or catch him off guard. Not even an unexpected attack. Or everything he planned to do to his queen. Many ideas had played in a loop in his mind as he accomplished his tasks. A slow smirk tugged at the corners of his mouth. Fuck, he couldn't wait to make her bleed. He halted in front of the guard.

"Sir," the soldier dipped his chin, acknowledging Jaq.

"Ensure the queen's ladies' maids do not enter her chambers until morning." While he didn't care what his men heard, he preferred no one walk in unannounced, interrupting them. Rumors regarding his relationship with Carter spread years ago. It didn't mean he had to confirm them.

"Yes, sir."

With a slight nod, Jaq clapped the male on the back of shoulder and waltzed past him. Light from the torches bounced off the stone walls, dancing with his shadow as he strode down the corridor. Not that it gave his presence away. His footsteps didn't even echo as he headed toward the queen's quarters. As he'd left hours ago, Carter should have spent much of that time just like he demanded.

Jaq slowed his pace and stopped in front of the queen's bedroom. Before entering, he listened for any slight tics or other indication that she'd failed to heed his command. The only sounds that came through the thick oak door were the faint rise and fall of her shallow breaths and the flames crackling in the fireplace. "Good girl," he murmured.

Gripping the metal door handle, he opened the door, stepped into the immense bedroom, and shut the door behind himself. His gaze fell to Carter, who sat on her knees, spread wide and her palms face up against her thighs. He swept his tongue across his bottom lip and completely drank her in.

Her dark-reddish-brown hair hung in loose ringlets over her shoulders, cascading down her back. She had nothing on save a black collar with heart-shaped rubies embedded in it. A metallic chain, fastened to the collar, draped the valley between her ample bosoms. *Fuck.* She looked like the sweetest, shiniest red apple sitting there waiting for him.

His eyes strayed to her slim stomach and over the curve of her hips. Oh, he had so many plans for her smooth flesh. Jaq unhooked the buttons of his vest as he took a step forward. "Look at me, little queen."

Her gaze lifted to meet his. Her hazel-brown eyes glazed with need.

"You look hungry, little queen." Perfect. The question lingering on the tip of his tongue wasn't necessary. Based on that look, she'd sat there long enough that the cold stone bit into her flesh. Just as he desired. Removing his vest, he tossed it aside, yanked the tunic over his head, and added it to the pile.

"Starving, Sir."

"I'm sure we can do something about that." Oh, yeah. They could definitely take care of her hunger. At least for starters. He undid the belt around his waist, popped the buttons on his leathers, freeing his erection, and stopped a few feet from where she kneeled. "But you weren't very good earlier. What do you think we should do about that? Or do you think I have punished you enough?"

Not that her answer mattered too much. Unless she used her safe word, he wasn't ready to let her up yet. She deserved to suffer a bit more. Though he wouldn't hold out forever. That didn't jibe with his plans.

"I have certainly endured more than enough punitive actions, Sir. Kneeling here for hours as you instructed. Is it not?" Her eyes sparkled mischievously as she tacked on, "Sir."

Just a small defiance, but oh, how she tested the waters. It was one of the many things he enjoyed about this dance between them. Jaq wrapped a hand around his cock and stroked his shaft. "Mmm… no. It isn't enough. You need a reminder that'll stick, little queen. Unacceptable behavior doesn't warrant a reward."

She took a cursory glance at his iron-hard arousal as his hand slid up and down his dick. Her tongue snaked out across her bottom lip. "You're right, Sir, but I have absolutely learned my lesson, Sir."

"Have you, now?" he groaned. Shit. He couldn't say what he enjoyed more. The way she held her breath as she watched every move he made. Or the slight trembling in her thighs as she kept her back ramrod straight and her hands still. It pleased him how she fought against her desires. Oh, yes. This was an excellent punishment.

Her fingers flexed a touch as she jutted her chin, meeting his gaze. "Yes, Sir. Please, may I have a taste, Sir? Please, Sir, don't deprive me."

Talk about a new level of begging. In all the years they'd been together, not once had she ever used 'Sir' so many times in one request. Regardless, he wasn't ready to give her what she wanted. Some denial would do her good. "You're not bereft of anything… yet."

"Please, Sir. What can I do to have a taste, Sir?" she rasped.

Oh, he could think of several things. At the top of the list: nothing. Another option: his claws buried in her shoulders. He intended to make her bleed. Although he didn't have to do that himself. The corner of his mouth curled. "Rake your nails across your thighs. Show me how badly you want my cock in your mouth, little queen." Otherwise, she could sit there and watch as he made himself come.

"Yes, Sir," Carter purred. She dug her fingernails into her skin and dragged them across her thighs. Crimson beaded in a line, staining her creamy flesh. A moan slipped from her mouth. Her gaze dropped to his cock as he stroked his shaft.

Oh, yes. That was exactly what he yearned to see, but he needed more. Much more. "Is that all?" Jaq grunted and increased the pace of his strokes. Fuck. If he kept this up, it wouldn't take much longer for him to come. "I thought you were starving."

"I am, Sir." She licked her pink lips. Her manicured nails bit into her flesh until blood welled under her fingertips. It slowly trickled down her delectable thighs.

His gaze dropped to the rivulet of red trailing her inner thigh. Jaq drew his lower lip in by his teeth, barely holding back a growl. *Fuck, yes.* It seemed she finally gave him what he wanted. Maybe he should return the favor. "That's my good girl." Releasing his erection, he strode forward and closed the distance between them. "Now show me just how hungry for me you really are because once I finish fucking your exquisite mouth, I'm gonna eat that sweet pussy." That wasn't all he planned.

Without uttering a word, her fingers skated across his throbbing shaft. She pushed up onto her knees, aggressively grabbed his cock, and licked the swollen head.

His eyes rolled back as her mouth tightly encircled his shaft, and she explored his length with her tongue. "Fuck," Jaq groaned. He gripped her shoulders, his claws piercing the soft skin of her back. It took every ounce of control he mustered not to fuck her mouth. They'd get there, but not yet. For the moment, he allowed her to set their pace. Soon enough, he'd do everything that he desired and more.

Carter's hands trailed over his hips. The skin-to-skin contact heightened the sensations of her tongue as she twirled it around his aching dick. Fuck. She was driving him crazy; each motion drawing him closer to the edge. As she slid her palms over his ass, he cupped the back of her head and thrust his cock deep into her mouth until she gagged on his length.

The slight droplets of water prickling the corners of her eyes called out a deep rumble of satisfaction. Not that she noticed it or cared. She dug her nails hard into his ass cheeks and sucked her cheeks in, tightening her mouth around his shaft. "Fuucckk," he hissed. A jolt of pleasure shot through him, dragging him to the brink.

Losing all sense of restraint, Jaq drew his hips back and plunged his raging erection into the sweet depths of her mouth. Her fingers clenched, gripping his behind harder. Clamping his hand on the back of her head, he picked up his rhythm. With each thrust, her tongue made circular motions up and down his length, taking complete possession of him.

Every nerve-ending in his body fired. His balls tightened. Jaq roared as he reached the verge of a massive release. An incredible orgasm shot up the length of his cock and exploded out of him. Carter's mouth suctioned tight around him. The corner of his lips curled as she milked him dry. Not that it affected his erection. He didn't lose a bit of his hardness.

"Good girl." Jaq stilled his hips, removed her hands from his ass, and withdrew his cock. Fuck. Even though he just came, the way she looked at him right now only heightened his arousal.

Her honey-brown eyes blazed with hunger. She swept a delicate finger across her lower lip and sucked it clean. "Thank you, Sir."

Leaning down, he pressed his lips to hers and devoured her mouth with deep, sweeping strokes of his tongue. *Fuck.* She tasted absolutely divine. A deep rumble resounded in his chest as he released the kiss. Their gazes locked on one another. He was beyond ready to eat the fuck out of that pussy. Jaq ran his fingers across her collarbone, over her breast, and gave the long chain hanging down a slight tug. "Climb on the bed. Get on all fours. Ass high."

"Yes, Sir." Mischief danced in her eyes. Without hesitation, she rose to her feet and sashayed toward the bed.

As much as he enjoyed watching her hips swing from side to side with each step she took, he had to collect a few things. He crossed to the dresser against the wall nearest the door, grabbed the empty torch holder, and pulled it forward. The wall turned, rotating backward, and revealed all the toys they enjoyed utilizing during their playtime.

Jaq scanned the various items hanging on the wall. His gaze flicked from a set of ropes to the silk scarves to the leather cuffs. Each had their own pros and cons for use. He curled his fingers around the thick, braided fibers of the ropes. They'd generate the right amount of friction and discomfort. What else should he include for the night's festivities? He eyed the ball gags. While they'd used them in the past, her earlier begging hadn't pleased him at all. A lesson on groveling would remind his little queen what he considered a *genuine* cry for mercy. So, nothing that would muffle her sounds of pleasure or pleas for release. He stole a glance at that round derriere of hers. There were other ways she could atone for her defiance.

Returning his attention to the wall, he eyed the other numerous items on display—paddles, nipple clamps, eye masks, and more. Each item was something they'd used in prior sessions. Nothing called to him right then. He clutched the rope a little tighter. Sometimes modest worked just as well as anything else. The corner of his mouth lifted as he strode over to the bed. Stopping at the edge, he trailed his fingers down her back and squeezed her soft bottom. Carter moaned. Oh, yes. He required nothing beyond the rope.

"Mmm, I'm going to devour you," Jaq said as he moved around the bed. He tied one end of each of the ropes to the metal rings attached to the bed posts. Then he wrapped the other end of the four ropes around her wrists and ankles, spreading her legs and arms wide. Once he had her situated to his liking, he stood behind her and admired his handiwork. She was on full display, ready for his use.

A raspy breath left Carter's mouth as she tugged on the cords around her wrists. "Fuck, yes."

He growled as her scent thickened in his nostrils. Her arousal was the sweetest aroma he'd ever scented. He was eager as fuck to get his mouth on her. First, he had to set the rules because, once he started, there was no stopping. "Prove to me you can beg properly." As he spoke, he gingerly ran his fingers up and down her spine and across her ass. Lifting his hand, Jaq brought his palm down against her flesh. A loud *thwack* echoed off the walls. "Your earlier performance was abysmal. Until I hear you *truly* beg, you cannot come. Understood?"

"Yes, Sir," she purred.

Leaning over her body, he glided his claws down her back and splayed his fingers across her slim waist. He pressed his erection against her ass. Not that he planned to fuck her just yet. At least not before he got a taste of what he really wanted. Jaq nipped her ear with his fang and whispered, "That's my good little queen."

On a moan, Carter jerked the ropes a bit as she arched her back and ground her ass against him.

"Is my little queen eager for something?" Regardless of what she wanted, he refused to hurry. He preferred to take his time with everything. The longer she held her release back, the stronger it would be. As he trailed his fingers over her curves toward her thighs, he swept her hair aside and skimmed his fangs down the back of her neck.

"Yes, please," she groaned. "Stop teasing me and either fuck me hard or eat my pussy." Glancing over her shoulder at him, she licked her lips and rubbed her ass against his cock. "*Sir,*" Carter tacked on.

Jaq lifted his gaze to hers. "Stop teasing, huh?" Oh, she didn't know how badly he could tease her. A devilish grin crept across his face. "I think you misunderstood me. I'm going to devour every inch of you." With a low snarl, he sank his fangs into her side and dug his claws into her inner thigh.

"Fuck!" The threads of the rope scraped against the satin sheets. "Again, please, Sir."

Oh, yes. That was a much better response. She'd quickly gotten the hint of what would get them both what they yearned for. He'd happily comply with her plea. He swept his tongue across his bite mark, cleaned the crimson dotting her flesh, and inched further down her body. Drawing his hand back, his palm connected with one ass cheek as his fangs pierced the other.

"Gods, yes!" Carter cried out in pure ecstasy. Her toes curled as she yanked on the rope tied to her ankles. "More, please, Sir. Can I please have some more, Sir?"

That she could. Jaq massaged the cheek he'd just swatted and glided his long fingers toward that sweet spot. Before he gave her exactly what she yearned for, he needed to push her closer to the edge. Switching sides, with his free hand, he spanked her other cheek and bit the opposite side.

"Oh, gods, please, Sir. I need more. Please, give me more. Please, Sir."

Fuck, he rather enjoyed the way she pleaded with him. Something she needed to give him in spades before he allowed her to come. That wasn't she asked for, was it? Jaq brushed his fingertips across the outer lips of her pussy. His tongue stroked the new bite mark. He growled as the sweetness of her blood hit his tastebuds. Despite the number of times he'd sunk his fangs into her flesh, he hadn't done it nearly enough. Without a second thought, he bit her ass cheek again and pierced her skin with his teeth.

Carter gasped as her thighs tensed. She rocked her hips, pressing her pussy harder against his finger. "Oh, gods, please fuck me," she begged. "Please, please, Sir."

His cock throbbed with need. If he was a weaker man, he might give in, but he was a dragon. And he didn't succumb easily or quickly. Driving his fangs harder into her ass cheek, he sucked on her flesh and lapped at the blood filling his mouth. Jaq slipped a finger into the moist, warm folds between her thighs. *Fuck, yes.* She was so damn wet for him.

"Yes, please, Sir! Please… please… I need your tongue… I need your cock. Please, Sir, please give it to me." She groaned as she clenched her pussy around his finger. "Please, please, Sir. Oh, gods, please."

When she pleaded with him like that, how could he deny her further? He tore his fangs from her ass. His tongue snaked out across his lips, catching the droplets of blood that trickled down his chin. "Fuck, you're delicious." His gaze fell to her delicate softness. He was about to have more of her on his tongue. Dropping to his knees, Jaq drove his tongue into the cleft between her legs. Every part of his body hummed with pleasure.

"Oh, god!" Carter bucked forward. The satin sheets scrunched between her fingers as she closed her fists around them. "Please, Sir, please give me more. Gods, I need to come. Please, please, can I come?"

Not yet. Not that he had to say that. He'd made the rules quite clear, and he'd only just gotten started. It didn't even matter that his balls ached. The pain only urged him to plunge his tongue deeper inside her folds, exploring every inch of her pussy as it belonged to him. Because it did. He wrapped his hands around her thighs, gripping them tightly, and drew her closer to him.

Her back bowed as a small, breathless whisper escaped her lips. Carter repeatedly mumbled 'please' as her nails scraped against the sheets. Her thighs quivered under his touch. "Please, may I come? Please, please, may I come?"

Fire singed every nerve-ending. A blaze burned through him and shot straight to his rock-hard cock. He desperately needed to bury himself inside of her, but first, he needed to consume her. The rest could wait a bit more. Jaq pressed his thumb to her nub, stroking it in slow circles, and removed his tongue from her pussy. "Come for me, little queen. And don't stop."

"Oh, gods," she sighed in relief. "Wait, what?"

His only response—he fused his mouth to her slick folds and dipped his tongue into her hot center. Carter had heard him. She screamed in delight as an intense orgasm exploded all over the length of his tongue. Her body quaked under him as he relentlessly devoured her. Though he didn't stop. Even once her release ended, he kept going. What little she gave him wasn't enough. He refused to stop until he completely satiated his beast. Hours could pass for all he cared. The more she gave him, the more he desired.

Jaq swallowed every release of hers that gushed into his waiting mouth. He lost count of the number of times he made her come. Or how long he went at her. Nor did it matter. He wasn't yet sated, but his erection fiercely ached. After he gave himself a small reprieve, he'd return to consuming her. With the tip of his tongue, he licked the last of her sweetness and stood. "Mmm, so delicious." Gripping his shaft, he pressed the head of his cock to her entrance. With a single swing of his hips, he sank into the cleft between her thighs. "Fuck," he groaned.

"Gods, yes," Carter panted. She balled the sheets up in her hands as her body lowered, allowing him to penetrate her deeper. Her back arched as she ground her pussy back against his shaft. "Holy shit. Gods, fuck me hard, please, Sir."

"With pleasure." His hands anchored to the rounded curve of her hip. His claws pierced her creamy flesh as he pummeled her without taking the time to build a steady rhythm. Although the ropes around her ankles restricted her movements, she still met him stroke for stroke. Their bodies slapped loudly against one another. It didn't take either of them long to peak. Her hot, wet sheath clamped onto his cock. Her scream had his body thrumming with rapt intoxication.

"Fuck, yes!" he growled. Her thighs tensed as a massive release gushed out of her, drenching his dick and their legs. It set off his own orgasm. His balls tightened and a colossal release punched up the length of his shaft. Jaq roared, echoing off the walls as he pounded into her. The coppery scent of her blood intensified the pleasure coursing through his body. It went on in an endless wave as they rode out their mutual orgasm.

Carter sagged beneath him. Only the sound of their ragged breaths filled the room. Her eyes brimmed with pure sexual bliss.

His gaze flicked over the bite marks, bruises, streaks of crimson, and sweat that beaded across her skin. "Fuck, you look exquisite." And well used. The corner of his mouth lifted. "I'm gonna add so much more before the night's over. Because we're far from finished, little queen."

For the first time in years, he really had her within his grasp. She belonged to him. And he fully planned to own every part of her over and over until she begged him for mercy. Something he wouldn't relinquish easily.

Lewis stared at Alicia. Yeah, like he wanted to share that little tidbit.

Telling her that part of his history gave too much away. Though she had one point; they needed to work together. As much as he despised it, he couldn't get out of Wonder without her assistance. A witch had drawn him into this magical place and a witch had to get him out.

Lucky him.

His eyes narrowed. Something appeared off with her. Alicia scanned the room, almost as if she saw something. Though she said nothing. Was that what had brought her in here? He hadn't encountered anything, but rumors suggested witches saw things others couldn't. He didn't know much about her kind. Other than they had their own factions, similar to how his species had packs. Though his pack mostly kept to itself. They only interacted with one other pack on a semi-regular basis. Simply because they had a doctor. Last he knew, anyway. That could've changed since his… disappearance. "You first."

Her pink lips twisted into a sneer. "You seriously want to play that game?" She waved a dismissive hand at him. "Nevermind. Forget I asked. You do you and I'll do me. We'll see who gets out of here first." With a derisive shake of her head, she spun around on the back of her heel and started toward the hallway.

Shit. Two choices lay before him. Either he took the higher road and answered her or he allowed her to walk off for the second time this evening. Neither seemed like a good idea, but only one made his blood boil. Could he answer her without providing all the details? Lewis scrubbed a hand across his face and raked his fingers through his hair. "An enchanted egg… I think."

Alicia halted in her steps. Turning around, she cocked her head at him. "What did it look like? The egg."

Strange question. Unless… No. Impossible. The egg couldn't have brought her here. Could it? "It was yellow with crystals on it. Like one of those fancy ones you see in high-end stores."

Her gaze dropped to the floor. As her eyes lifted back to him, she stepped forward. "How did you get it?"

"Honestly, I don't know." It wasn't much of an answer. Hell, it wasn't one at all, but it was the best he had.

As she lifted her chin, her piercing blue eyes hardened. "Are you fucking kidding me? Don't jerk me around. How did it come into your possession?"

Letting out a heavy sigh, he propped his hands on his hips. "I'm serious, Alicia." He rolled his shoulders. *Shit.* Her name came out of its own volition. Damn, he really enjoyed saying it. Shaking the shivers from his body, he focused on their conversation. "I don't know. I just woke up one morning and it was in my room." Maybe if he had, he could've escaped Wonder sooner. "Why does it matter?"

Gripping her wrist with her hand, she tapped her fingers against her arm. Her lips pinched together and she blew out a deep breath. "It just helps to know its origins. The more I can learn about it, the more I can narrow down the spell that pulled us in here. So I can figure out how to get us out."

Lewis folded his arm across his chest. None of that sounded useful toward an escape. Gods, please don't let that hinder them. While he could get them to a certain point, he'd never gotten beyond the worebeore. Even if they slipped past it, they still had to face the Red Queen. "Please tell me you can get us free."

"If we can find my grimoire, then yes."

"Right. Your spell book or whatever." He frowned. Holloway didn't mention it when the creature had sent him to her. That didn't mean much. That cat left things out regularly.

"Yeah," Alicia muttered as she gripped the back of her neck. "I had it when the egg pulled me in so it should've come with me. But I didn't see it when I came around. That's why I need you. Obviously, you're not from this world, but you've been here long enough to know it."

Just as he hadn't given her a lot of information, she had provided none, either. Nothing in her statement told him how the egg captured her. Or how it ended up in her hands. If he asked, would she tell him? Unlikely. Witches used people and lied for their own gain. He expected she'd try to do the same. Not that he'd allow her. It began with getting some truth.

"How'd you get the egg?"

"My grandmother gifted it to me. And all I know about how she got it is that someone located it for her."

His jaw slackened. Someone gave it to her? Why would they do that? That couldn't be right. Except, nothing in her facial expression or eyes indicated that she'd lied. Shit. Did he trust her? What would it cost him to take her at her word? His freedom. His sanity. Everything.

Alicia raised an eyebrow at him. "What? Didn't think I'd answer?"

No, but he kept that thought to himself. Lewis dragged a hand down his face and let out a soft breath. "You said you had a proposition."

"Yes. You serve as a guide and I'll get us out."

His eyebrows drew together as he gawked at her. Maybe he hadn't given her enough time to lay it all out. He waited a beat. Nothing but silence greeted him. "That's it? That simple? One service for another?"

"Did you expect an entire list of rules or some shit?" She frowned. "What kind of person do you take me for? Or do you just not trust me?"

Of course, he didn't. She was a witch. He opened his mouth and snapped it shut. For some unexplainable reason, he couldn't verbalize his thoughts. *Alright. Then try this another way.* "We don't exactly know one another."

"Fair enough." Pursing her lips, she interlocked her hands together at the small of her back and walked toward him. "Then perhaps it would be best if we set a few ground rules. Like… we are completely honest with one another."

Could he agree to that? Possibly. He could be honest without revealing everything. "We don't go into anything half-assed." If she charged forward or reacted without thinking, she would draw unwanted attention to them. They didn't need that.

"We have to agree on every plan," Alicia replied.

His heart skipped a beat as he narrowed his gaze at her. Some part of that bothered him. What if she wasn't a strategist? Or too soft-hearted? Shit. What other choice did he have? Even if he got past the guards and made it to the Red Queen's fortress, he required a witch to defeat her.

What had he gotten himself into? His only means of escape. "Fine. We'll start with getting you better clothes. You need to blend in better."

Stopping a few feet from him, Alicia nodded and held out her hand. "Then we have a deal."

Lewis cocked an eyebrow at her outstretched hand. *Fuck it.* He was in it now. Too late to turn back. "Deal." He clasped her hand, palm-to-palm. Their gazes locked on one another. Something surged through him as they shook. He swallowed, beating the tingling sensation back, and quickly dropped her hand.

Neither of them uttered a word for several moments. Their quickened breaths and the sound of the crackling flames filled the room. Alicia cleared her throat. "Um, do you, uh, have something I can change into for the night? So, I can get out of this?"

Were her eyes always that blue? They were exquisite, sparkling like sapphires. Warmth flooded him. He slowly lifted his hand. What the fuck was he doing? Replaying her questions, he gripped the back of his neck. "Uh, yeah, sure." Shit. He only possessed male clothing, but he supposed they could make it work. At least for tonight. "Follow me." Stepping around her, Lewis headed toward the bedroom.

"You mean to tell me I could've found something already?" she called out as she trailed him.

"Sort of. What I have is made for me, but my tunic should suffice." He refused to think about what it wouldn't cover. None of that needed to dance across his brain. Nope. He rolled his shoulders and rubbed at the slight ache in his chest. *Focus, asshole. Get it together.* This woman was just a means to an end. Nothing more.

"I'll take whatever you have. I can make it work."

Lewis stole a glance at her over his shoulder. He imagined she could. "Oh?" Fuck. Why had he asked for more details? They weren't important.

"Shrinking spell. Even if it's too big, I can make it fit." A brief smile fluttered across her face. "Do you have something to eat?"

Right. Magic. How could he have forgotten? "Uh, yeah." He entered the bedroom, strode over to the closet, and located a pair of old leathers, a shirt, and a pair of boots. Turning around, he held them out to her. "Here."

"Thanks," she said as she accepted the items, clutching them against her body. Her gaze flicked from him to the door.

"Oh. Right. I'll… uh, I'll just be in the kitchen when you're ready." His feet remained glued to the floor. What the fuck was he doing? Why was he just standing here? Privacy. He needed to give her privacy. One foot in front of the other. That simple. Yet his body wouldn't budge. It took physical effort to force his body out of the room. Lewis shut the door behind himself. Sighing heavily, he leaned against the wall. Fuck, he seriously had to get her out of his head. It didn't matter how attractive he found her. She was still a witch. Regardless of their deal, he couldn't trust her.

Ever.

CHAPTER
six

ALICIA SURVEYED THE colorful awnings as they weaved in and out of the crowd. Everything about this place was strange. A step out of the past. The males sported leather trousers and cotton tunics, while the females wore long dresses and hooded cloaks. Except for those of a higher stature. Those women adorned themselves in silks and satins. Various sparkling jewels covered them from head to toe.

Thankfully, between the attire she borrowed from Lewis and how well her spell held, she blended in better than she had last night. Though it surprised her that her magic hadn't lost its spark. Just in case, she kept her arms wrapped around her stomach. "Where are we going?"

They rounded a corner and started down a back alley. "There." Lewis pointed to the red-brick building with a bright-yellow door.

She cocked an eyebrow at the crooked sign hanging above the red-and-yellow-checkered awning. "O'Malley's Apparel and Accessories." It had a name. That was something. A few of the shops didn't even have that. Their posts only identified them as bakery, blacksmith, and butcher.

"Just keep your head down and let me do the talking. Got it?"

"Afraid I'll give something away?" She snorted. Just because she required some help, it didn't make her incapable of taking care of business. "I can hold my own in a conversation, even small talk. Or shopping and negotiating."

Lewis halted and narrowed his golden-brown eyes at her. A muscle in his jaw ticked. He pointed a finger at her. "Not like here, princess. Let me do the talking. Understood?"

Her heart pounded so loudly in her ears she thought she might go deaf. A strange tingling sensation gripped her body like a vise. Shit. That forceful look on his face did something to her. Alicia swallowed the moisture in her mouth. "Got it."

"Good. Let's go." Scanning their surroundings, he started forward.

It unnerved her the way he continuously checked things out. She couldn't look less like herself than she did right then. Did he think the soldiers would recognize her? Even with her hair braided back as she'd done before they left. "This place is safe, right?"

"One of the safest in Thornkeep."

"I thought we were in Wonder. Or is that another part of the… queen's domain or whatever?" Or was that the name of the bazaar they had strolled through over the last few minutes? She saw nothing denoting a name, but that meant little.

Lewis lowered his voice as he spoke. "All of it is under the Red Queen's rule. Thornkeep is the local town. And one of the few places where those against her openly hide. Most of her opposition shrouds themselves."

"Oh." He'd mentioned the Red Queen a few times now, but hadn't shared anything substantial regarding the female. Frowning, Alicia grabbed his arm and stopped him. "Is she really as bad as you're making her out to be?"

"She's the worst of the worst." With a heavy sigh, Lewis propped his hands on his hips and glanced over her shoulder. His gaze dropped to her as he curled his fingers around her elbow and ushered her onward. "We need to keep moving."

Right. They were being hunted, but he couldn't keep things about this place from her forever. It hadn't occurred to her to ask questions during their trek through the woods earlier. She had to find out at some point. Right then seemed better than later or never. "Fine, but we will talk about this."

Lewis grunted and muttered something imperceptible under his breath. "Just not when we're out in the open like this. We don't need the inquisitive overhearing our conversation."

Who the fuck was he talking about? She peered around at the assorted shoppers. None of them stood out to her. So what if one or two gossiped with one another? That appeared normal. Alicia opened her mouth—

"Before you ask, yes, we're being watched," he stated through gritted teeth. "Now head into the shop before I throw you over my shoulder and carry you in there."

A shiver shot down her spine. He seriously needed to stop spouting shit like that. "You're an ass," she snapped. Jerking the oak door open, she stomped across the threshold and disappeared inside the store. They had to escape Wonder quickly. She couldn't take much more of him or his arrogance.

A red-headed male standing behind a nearby counter flashed a pearly-white smile in her direction. "Hello. Welcome to O'Malley's." His gaze flicked past her and his smile faltered slightly. "Lewis. What brings you in here?"

"We came for a few items, Jimmy."

The male canted his head. "'*We?*' Don't tell me you're with this lovely creature. She's far too gorgeous to be with the likes of you."

Glaring at the guy, Lewis folded his arms across his pecs. "Are you done? Or do I need to get your brother out here to service us?"

"Be my guest." Jimmy snorted, stepped around the counter, propped against it, and draped one ankle over the other. "Better yet… hey, Paddy. We got company."

"Oh, yeah? Who is it?" Another guy exited a back room and joined them. "Well, I'll be damned. If it isn't the—"

"Can we cut the shit?" Lewis quipped, cutting the guy off.

Alicia scrutinized both males. Shit. They looked like twins. They each sported short, dark-red hair and bright-amber eyes. That didn't include the matching sharp jawline. The two of them almost reminded her of her twin cousins, Ruby and Rain. Especially how they all spoke about her as if she wasn't standing right here in front of them.

She could've handled this herself. If only she hadn't idiotically agreed to let Lewis take care of things. Not that she had to keep to that. He got a whole lot of nowhere. If he didn't get them on track in the next sixty seconds, she would take over. Whether or not he liked it.

"We've just never seen you with such a gorgeous woman before," Paddy said.

"Well, any woman," Jimmy corrected.

"So, it's only natural that we would want to know something about her," Paddy countered.

"At least an introduction."

If those two continued with the back-and-forth testosterone-fueled rhetoric, she might set something on fire. She gave him plenty of time to handle the situation. Time they did things her way. Her forehead creased as her mouth downturned. Clasping her hands at the small of her back, Alicia strolled around the twin males. "I thought this was a place of professionalism. A safe space." She stole a sidelong glance at Lewis. "That is what he told me, but thus far, you both seem far more interested in *who* I am rather than providing service. Perhaps we should simply take our business elsewhere. There are other vendors who sell what we're looking for and who'd have fewer questions."

"No!" the two males interjected simultaneously.

"We meant no disrespect. Tell us whatever it is you need and we can provide it," Paddy stated.

"Yes, we apologize," Jimmy added. "It's unnecessary to go elsewhere."

Alicia flashed a smile at Lewis. See, she could be quite useful. "We require a few articles of clothing and a sturdy leather satchel. None of that cheap shit. I need something of quality." She eyed the various items in the shop. A few pieces stood out to her—a pair of brown-leather pants with a matching under-bust corset, a white tank-style peasant top, knee-high boots, and a set of bracers. Yeah, that should work. "I'll let you three haggle over the price." Taking off, Alicia collected what she spotted. And thank Lilith, they had some undergarments, too. Not much of a selection, but she'd deal with what was available. "Is there a place in the back that I can change?"

"Um, yes, of course. I'll show you." Jimmy led her toward the only dressing room in the back of the shop.

Tugging the curtain shut, Alicia set the pile on a wooden bench and stared at it. She'd never worn anything like it before, but whatever. At least all of this would fit properly. Changing would give Lewis the time to gather the intelligence they required to locate her grimoire. Or so she hoped. Because without it, they were flying blind.

Lewis stared at Alicia as she disappeared into the changing room. Grinding his jaw, he cracked his neck. She didn't listen to him at all. One simple instruction—let him handle the twins. Yet, she went off and inserted herself into the conversation. Luckily, it benefited them. He clenched his hands and released them. Her defiance shouldn't affect him like this. Fuck. He had to get this woman out of his life. And whatever this… feeling was out of his system.

"Interesting," Paddy snickered.

Without taking his gaze away from the back room, he cocked an eyebrow at the male. What the fuck was he prattling on about now? "What is?"

"You're attracted to her, but you're fighting it. Or at least you're trying."

His eyes snapped to Paddy. Where the fuck had he gotten that idea? It was complete bullshit. Lewis scoffed. "Your sight must be going." Yeah, he had eyes. She was gorgeous. Who wouldn't see that? Even these two morons saw it. That didn't mean he felt anything toward her.

"Keep telling yourself that."

Shaking his head, he slashed his hand through the air. He had other things to worry over rather than a pointless argument. "Where's Holloway?

I need to talk to him."

Paddy shrugged. "Your guess is as good as mine. He comes and goes at his leisure, but you know that."

Blowing out a heavy breath, he scrubbed a hand across his face. Why the fuck had he bothered coming here? Right. It was the only place he'd find the damn cat and Alicia required clothes. His ears twitched at the shuffled steps of one twin. Lewis lifted his gaze and watched Jimmy as the male crossed the shop, retrieved a cloak that matched the color of Alicia's eyes, and returned to the changing room.

Jimmy cleared his throat. "Excuse me, Miss. I have something else that would look wonders with your attire."

"Oh?" Alicia called out. "Um, can you pass it to me?"

"Of course." Jimmy peered over his shoulder at Lewis. A low yelp escaped the male's mouth.

What the fuck? A throaty, guttural sound reverberated around the shop. Where the hell was that noise coming from? Lewis pegged Jimmy with a hard stare. The male quickly covered his eyes and held the cloak out. "Here you are, Miss."

Fuck. The snarl came from him. Great way to prove Alicia didn't appeal to him in the slightest. Just fucking great.

"What the…?" Her words trailed off. The curtain shifted slightly as she poked her head out. "For the love of Lilith." Alicia grabbed the cloak and retreated into the dressing room.

"No," Paddy drew out the word. "You're not attracted to her at all."

His jaw clenched at the obvious sarcasm in the male's comment. Lewis shifted his weight from one foot to the other. One swing. It would only take one hit to Paddy's jaw. "Keep it up and you're gonna kiss the floor."

"Now, now. Don't go bloodying the twins in the shop," a voice uttered from beside him. An opaque form slowly became visible.

Not that he needed it to confirm it was Holloway. "About damn time."

"I had to ensure your princess got everything she required," his baritone voice carried through the air.

Lewis balled his hands into fists. This damn cat needed to quit bouncing around. As long as he got what he required, the reason mattered little. "Whatever. We have to talk. Privately." At least as much as they could.

"Patrick," Holloway started. "Please fetch a satchel for the young lady from the back."

The male rolled his eyes. "Sure." With a faint snort, Paddy walked off.

Cocking an eyebrow, Lewis stared after the male as he disappeared into the back room. He did a double take and gripped the back of his neck. Nothing ever happened that easily. Unless… of course. Narrowing his eyes at Holloway, Lewis snickered. "You already know what we seek."

A pearly-white smile flashed across the cat's pudgy face. "The heart of the matter, which has certainly fractured. The road will be difficult, but I can provide consult. Take the starry route, of that I am firm, for it will lead you to the blue worm." Holloway's gaze flicked toward the changing area before he disappeared.

What the…? Fuck! The cat gave him nothing other than a damn riddle. And what the fuck…? His eyes fell on Alicia. Lewis swallowed as he drank in the sight of her. She looked utterly exquisite. Her silky blonde hair fell back over her shoulder, while a few loose strands framed her angelic face. The brown corset she had on hugged her waist, emphasizing her hourglass figure. With how she'd tucked the peasant top into the leather pants, it perfectly accentuated her long legs. And Holloway was right about the cloak. Not only did it compliment her features, but it made her look like a deadly huntress.

Alicia blinked as he gawked at her. "What? Is something out of place? I really thought I got this tied right."

"It's…" Lewis swallowed again and cleared his throat. "You're perfect."

"He's quite right, madame." A wide grin spread across Jimmy's face. "That cloak ties it all together rather splendidly."

"Yes, it does," Paddy tacked on as he joined them and held out a dark-brown side bag. "I believe this should meet your desires."

Accepting the knapsack, Alicia inspected it. She turned it over, ran her fingers along the seams, and checked out the inside. "Yeah. This is perfect." Her sapphire-blue eyes flicked between them. "Did you three agree on a price?"

The brothers exchanged a look. "It's on the house, madame," Paddy stated.

"Really?" Alicia beamed. Delight danced in her eyes. "That's rather kind of you both. Thank you."

"It's our pleasure," the twins replied simultaneously.

Lewis held his hand out to her. "Come on. Let's get moving. We're burning daylight." Not that he had a clue regarding the direction they should take. Maybe if he shared the limerick with Alicia, she could help him decipher it. As if he had another choice.

The smile on her face wavered. Silence stretched between them. Her jaw slackened and her gaze fixated on him. Hesitantly, Alicia took a step forward, closing the distance between them. Her brows drew together. Something flickered across her face, but he couldn't get a bead on it. Alicia dropped her gaze to his outstretched hand, but she didn't take it. "Yeah. Right." Glancing away, she moved around him and headed toward the door.

What the fuck? Propping a hand on his hip, Lewis lowered his head and gripped the back of his neck. He meant nothing by it. Right? No, of course not. That was the last thing on his mind. Hitching his shoulders up, he shook off his disappointment and trailed after her.

Alicia pushed the door open. "You find anything out?"

"Well, I got something. Not sure it'll be helpful, though." Or that they'd figure out whatever crap Holloway had spewed at him. Unless it was just useless drivel intended to delay them. Which made even less sense, given what the cat had shared with him yesterday.

"What does that mean?"

As their feet hit the dirt path of the alleyway, the sun beat down on them. The air turned rich and fragrant, filled with the scent of yeasty breads and local spices. Although they'd eaten prior to leaving his cabin, his stomach rumbled.

"What's going on there?" Alicia gestured to a crowd gathered in the central part of the market ahead of them.

"Shit." He grabbed her hand. "We need to go. Now." Stealing a quick glance, Lewis witnessed a set of guards escort two females on the stage. Yep. Definitely time to get out of here.

"Not until you explain." Glowering at him, she jerked free from his grasp.

Behind them, the throng of people gathered chanted. Something he'd heard far too many times to count. Nothing he wanted to think about right then. "It's a hanging." He leaned in close. "Of witches."

"What?" Alicia spun around on the back of her heel, facing the back of the crowd. "That's not right. They're not witches. We have to do something."

"The only thing we can do is leave." Before the guards caught sight of them. There was only so much he could do to protect her with the number of people bustling around them. "So, let's go."

"No," she asserted. "I won't stand by while innocent women are slaughtered." Jumping forward, she quickly put a few paces between them.

"Alicia," he snapped. *Damn it!* This woman was going to be the death of him. As he darted after her, he caught some kind of intonation on the wind. It was in some foreign language, but it obviously came from her. Lewis grasped her hand. Not that she stopped whatever spell she conjured.

A guard cast a look in their direction. "Witch!" the male screamed and pointed at her. "Get them!"

"Shit." Time to go. Without a second thought, he took her hand in his and dragged her in the shop's direction. There was a side alley they could dip down. Not that it would entirely get them out of this mess.

"What are you doing?" Alicia hollered. "I'm not done!"

"Yes, you are, princess!" Even if he had to throw her over his fucking shoulder. Heavy footsteps pounding against the ground sounded behind them. Lewis glanced over his shoulder. Several guards were hot on their trail.

"Let go of me!" While she tried to free herself from his grip, he just tightened the hold he had on her, refusing to let go. "I can help! I can—"

"Cause more problems," he snapped. He didn't give a fuck what she had convinced herself she could handle. If she hadn't intervened in the first place, they wouldn't be running. Darting toward to the left, they almost clipped the corner of a building as he dragged her along. He sized up the numerous rickety, wooden stalls they passed, searching for one they could cut through for a simple escape.

"Fuck you! I tried to save them! If you would just fucking listen…" she grumbled.

A sharp pain prickled his fingers. At first, it felt like nothing more than an annoying insect bite. Except the sensation intensified and shot up his palm. Yanking his hand back, he dropped Alicia's wrist and came to an abrupt halt. *What the fuck?* Lewis flicked his gaze from his hand to Alicia. Had she done it on purpose?

Defiance twisted her pretty mouth into a sneer as she thrust her chin, lifting her head high. She glared at him, daring him to challenge her. Spinning on the back of her heel, her long blonde braid flipped over her shoulder. Alicia rose her hands in the air, palms out, and blasted a wall of fire at the guards.

Flames licked at their flesh as their agonizing screams filled the air. Shoppers and vendors alike scampered, trying to get away from the blaze as it consumed one soldier after another. The acrid stench of burned flesh hit his nostrils. Scrunching his nose, Lewis grabbed the crook of Alicia's arm. "Let's go."

Whether it was a good thing or not, he didn't know, but at least this time, she didn't fight him. Instead, she trailed after him as he raced toward another pathway ahead. Their feet kicked up sand with each step they took along the uneven dirt road. As they rounded another corner, he spotted the sewer entrance close by.

A short distance stood between them and the access point. They were almost out of the bazaar. Out of his periphery, he caught a flash of red and black. His eyes narrowed. *Shit.* In one swift move, Lewis turned, drew the sword at his hip, and blocked an attack. A loud clank echoed as his blade connected with another. His gaze dropped to Alicia.

If the guard got any closer, she might've lost her head. Of all the males to escape incineration, it had to be someone he knew. Not that it would save the male's life. He'd happily end Eric's life, especially if it was the only way to protect Alicia. Baring his teeth, Lewis snarled at the piece of shit standing far too close for his liking. Fury blazed through him. As he shoved Eric back, Lewis stepped in front of Alicia and stared the soldier down.

Although Eric stumbled backward, he caught his footing and slowly circled Lewis. A sneer settled on his face as he pointed the sharp end of his blade at Lewis and Alicia. "Are you really protecting that witch? After everything the Red Queen has done for you?"

"You mean used me? Imprisoned me? Tortured me?" Lewis snapped. Alicia gasped behind him. The words tumbled out of his mouth before he could stop them. He hadn't intended to verbalize them. Not that he could take them back now. "Yes, I'll protect the witch. From every one of you. Every single fucking time." Not that he wanted to delve too much into those feelings.

"Then this will be your end. As well as hers." Letting loose a battle cry, Eric lunged at Lewis and swung his blade in a deadly arc.

Which Lewis easily parried. They'd done this song and dance before. Eric lost every single time in the past. The male had always been predictable in a fight. This was no different, but that worked in his favor. He needed to dispose of the soldier before any others joined the party and delayed their departure further.

He stole a sidelong glimpse out of his periphery, ensuring Alicia remained behind him and didn't involve herself. She'd already done that once. It didn't need to happen again. It was his job to keep her safe. As expected, the male lurched forward, nearly slicing his side. Lewis used Eric's momentum, drew a long dagger from the sheath on his right hip, spun around, and thrust it into the guy's belly.

A deep crimson color stained the white stripes in the soldier's garb. The sword he held fell from his hand, clattering to the ground as he hiccupped blood. His gaze dropped to the sharp blade. Without a second thought, Lewis jerked it free from the male's gut. Eric slumped to the uneven road, landing on his side with a soft thunk.

Wiping the blood from the steel across his leather pants, Lewis peered over at Alicia. "We need to go. Now." He shoved the double-edged blade back in its sheath, grabbed her hand, and dragged her toward the hidden hatch. They didn't need to wait around for the light in the soldier's eyes to dim. No one survived a strike like that.

No one.

CHAPTER
seven

ALICIA REGARDED LEWIS as he cracked his neck for the tenth time since they'd started down this tunnel. Lilith, that annoyed the shit out of her. What was with him? Between the way his broad shoulders hunched and his long strides, she might have pissed him off. Except that was absolutely ridiculous. Shaking the thoughts free, she drank in the labyrinth they slowly navigated their way through. It reminded her of an underground system dug by gophers. Not that she gave a lot of attention to the debris under their feet or the skritching sound of claws as they trekked along.

She'd tracked the unnatural silence between her and Lewis over the last fifteen minutes. And how his muscles strained against his skin with each long stride he took. Even the way he clenched and unclenched his fists, as if he replayed their narrow escape on an endless loop. "Are you upset with me?" The question popped out of her mouth before she could stop it. It was better they resolve the issue now, instead of letting it fester.

His gaze jerked in her direction. "You're damn right I am. You did the complete opposite of what we agreed to last night."

She arched a brow at him and folded her arms across her chest. "What are you talking about? We accomplished our task and got out of there."

At least, she assumed they'd completed the former. They hadn't actually discussed what information he'd gathered at the shop.

"That's beside the point," he retorted. "We agreed not to go into anything half-assed. That we'd decide together every step we took. Instead of heading my warning, you drew unnecessary attention our way."

Alicia opened her mouth and snapped it shut. Despite how much she wanted to argue with him, she couldn't. He had a point. She hadn't listened to his suggestion. Instead, she took the only recourse she believed was available. And she'd do it again. "Something we both handled… rather well, I might add."

"You don't get it," he snorted. "You could've gotten killed." Shaking his head, he scratched the back of his neck and blew out a heavy breath. "Yeah, it was only a handful of soldiers, but next time, it won't be." Tension filled his rough voice. There was something beyond the anger and frustration, but she couldn't quite identify it. Before she could respond, he huffed and stalked off.

Alicia's eyes bounced around the curved walls as she followed him, yet gave him the space he required. Could things have gone differently? She thought back over what had transpired in the bazaar. Not just the fire she'd magically conjured, but what she'd witnessed the soldiers do to those females. The way they'd traipsed them through the courtyard. It was like she'd been transported to the Salem witch trials. Something she never expected to see in her lifetime. Yeah, witches didn't get along with vampires or shifters and hunters claimed their lives, but she didn't expect to see anything like that.

And the control she managed over that spell… how the fuck had that occurred? Maybe her rage helped. The situation and Lewis' reaction to it infuriated her. Something that had faded since they'd climbed down into this… sewer? There was an overpowering stench of stagnant water. Unable to stand the quiet any longer, she blurted, "Is that common?"

"What?"

"Killing witches so… openly." Alicia frowned. That wasn't really accurate, though. "Well… claiming those women as witches. And killing them."

"Yes. Like when the Red Queen is trying to make a point." His eyebrows scrunched together. "Or she's trying to find someone."

"You mean like me?" Not that she had a clue how this so-called Red Queen would know a damn thing about her. Yeah, the queen's people chased her yesterday, but they couldn't have known she was a witch. Unless… they somehow identified the magic within her. Lewis figured that much out.

"Yeah." As he tilted his head, he slowed his pace. "How'd you know they weren't witches?"

"I didn't sense any magic in them." *Like with you,* she thought. She just hadn't determined if it meant he was a warlock or something else. While she'd never crossed paths with a vampire or shifter, she'd learned a little about them growing up. Either could walk around during the day. Sort of. Not all bloodsuckers could, but she didn't think he was one of them. And he definitely wasn't a hunter. They all knew how to recognize those fuckers.

"So… you get a feeling of some kind? Like with your book?"

"Something to that effect." It was a sixth sense. A tingle that started in her head and spread throughout her body. Like a minor hum underneath her skin. Though she didn't utter any of those descriptions. They all sounded strange, even to her ear, and she experienced it. Not that it mattered in the long run. The bottom line was that she could tell. "If they had any magic in them, I would've known."

Lewis tilted his head, curiosity raising his dark eyebrows. "But you still tried to save them? If they had magic, would you have reacted the same way?"

"Of course, I would. No one deserves to be slaughtered or harmed just for being different." What kind of question was that? Had he expected her to treat them as less than nothing just because they were human? That didn't seem right. Closing what little distance there was between them, she gripped his arm and stopped him. Her eyes locked on his. "I don't know what kind of experience you have with witches, but we believe in a balance. To me… all life is precious."

His face screwed up as he tore his gaze from hers, as if he had something to hide. Or he didn't believe her. "Right," he muttered and started forward again.

"Right," she echoed. What else could she say? Other than question his motives, but that hadn't gone over so well the first time around. Why would now make a difference? Blowing out a heavy sigh, Alicia jogged after him. Quickly catching up, she focused on the point of all of this. "Did you find out something about my grimoire?"

"Sort of." He cast a furtive glance at her. "I have an idea of where we need to go."

An idea? Alicia snickered. Hadn't he just chastised her for acting without consulting him? "Care to share? Or am I supposed to read your mind?"

Lewis rubbed his brow as his eyes darkened and his nose wrinkled. His expression tightened like he doubted her. Or maybe he didn't quite know what to believe. "I didn't think witches could do that," he commented.

"Are you sure?" she posed through a wide grin. It wasn't a power she possessed, but it amused her to let him think otherwise. At least a little.

"You're fucking with me." Letting out a low laugh, he smirked. "Alright. I deserved that. The one I consulted… part of what he said made no sense. What I have deciphered, we need to head to Fogley Forest. To meet up with another advisor."

Great. Just what they needed. Someone else to know of her existence and that she'd lost her grimoire. Alicia frowned. "Why don't you tell me what they said? Perhaps we can ascertain everything without talking to anyone else."

"Maybe." With a half-shrug, he recited, "'The heart of the matter, which has certainly fractured. The road will be difficult, but I can provide consult. Take the starry route, of that I am firm, for it will lead you to the blue worm.'"

What? Grimacing, she replayed the words of the riddle in her mind over and over. Talk about a brain-teaser. She tugged her braid over her shoulder and played with the ends of her blonde tresses as she chewed on the inside of her cheek. The first line could apply to several things—her betrothed, the grimoire, the egg's enchantment, her and Lewis' escape. Except, only one of them had fractured. Sort of. The second line seemed self-explanatory. But the third… she got nothing. "I'm not great with riddles. While I can extrapolate what part of it means, the first and last part… I don't know."

"I think they're a play on one another, just starting backward." He pointed to the sparkling ceiling above them as they walked. "Our starry route. A little on the nose, but this will lead us to Fogley Forest, where I believe we'll find our worm." The corner of his mouth lifted, offering the slightest hint of a smile. "As for the line before, it seems more overall to our journey, but I didn't expect it to be an easy one. The first part… that one I'm unsure about. Though, speaking to the worm might help with it."

Her brow furrowed. Alicia opened her mouth and snapped it shut. He couldn't mean a literal worm, could he? No. Not possible. Then again, she'd found herself inside of a magical artifact. Kind of took her whole understanding of the realm of possibility and tilted its axis. The simple truth—the impossible could be possible.

Jaq stood there monitoring the two soldiers as they hefted the female bodies into a large wooden wagon. He crouched down on the back of his haunches and lifted the rope, one end of it completely frayed. While he hadn't witnessed it, from what his men told him, they'd had to wrap a second noose around one of the witches' necks. *Had their witch tried to free them? Was that what led to the chase?*

The one that nearly ended in fucking disaster. Almost ruined his and Carter's carefully constructed plan. Tossing the strands aside, he rose to his full height of six foot four and followed the path those idiots had taken. His nose twitched as the acrid stench of burned flesh reached him, overriding the usual stale air, sweat, and dust that filled the bazaar. Not that it irritated him in the least. This wasn't his first experience with fire.

Though, normally he caused it.

Carter told him if this female was the witch they'd waited for all these decades, that she'd be extraordinary. That she was. That woman decimated five of his men in one fell swoop. Jaq eyed the remnants of the corpses laid out on the earth. *They'd done this shit to themselves.* He gave explicit instructions not to get too close if they gave chase. "Imbeciles," he mumbled.

Jaq stalked around the group, searching for anything left of the crispy critters. Nothing. Each soldier that had gotten caught in her blaze was nothing more than a charred cadaver. That witch's fire burned nearly as hot as his. Glancing at his subordinate, who wisely gave him space as he inspected the dead, Jaq gestured to the mess. "Get this shit cleaned up."

Not that he was finished.

One remained.

Biting back his annoyance with the fumbling fools, he proceeded to the last body. The male lay crumpled on the ground, one hand resting against his bloodied gut and the other sprawled against the dirt, inches from the hilt of a steel blade. It appeared as if the soldier reached toward it, seeking retribution as he took his last breaths. Yet failed.

It was a good thing the soldier was already dead. It saved him from killing the idiot. Especially as he expected their witness to confirm his suspicions. Dropping his hands to his hips, Jaq regarded the merchant who'd, according to his men, hidden in an adjacent alley and witnessed the encounter. "Tell me again what you saw."

"The soldier attacked the woman. The male with her stopped him. They argued, the two men. It appeared as if they knew one another, sire."

Of course, they did. Those two fought together a few times before Carter chained him up. Oh, how he missed playing with that piece of meat. "What was the quarrel?"

"The female, sire. The guard, he couldn't comprehend why the male chose her over the queen."

A beat passed as he waited for the merchant to continue. It took every ounce of control he had not to beat the witness senseless when the male said nothing further. "And?" Jaq prompted.

"He offered no explanation, but declared he would choose her every time."

Oh, he liked the direction this conversation took. Provided the witch's guardian was who he suspected. "Did you recognize the woman's protector?"

"Yes, sire. In these parts…" The shopkeeper peered around and lowered his voice, "He is known as *The Rabbit*."

"And they went this way?" Jaq strolled forward a few steps.

"Yes, sire. Under the ground."

A wide grin spread across Jaq's face. They'd gone toward Fogley Forest. No doubt seeking the grimoire. And they were together. Just as fate demanded. "Perfect."

As they exited the underground tunnel, leaving the lingering stench of stale water behind, Lewis inhaled a deep breath of the clean forest air. Even the sight of the towering trees swaying around them seemed to breathe new life into him. Their branches twisted and gnarled like grasping fingers that welcomed him back. That was the way of the forest. It was home. Though it wasn't the only thing that affected him, was it? He shot a cursory glance in Alicia's direction as they started forward.

Several unspoken questions danced in those bright-blue orbs of hers. Her lack of response surprised him. Whether she had no desire to ask or simply overlooked his earlier words, he didn't know. He hadn't meant to admit any of it. But something triggered inside of him the moment he'd placed himself between her and that strike.

Not that he'd change it.

Protecting her had suddenly become his number one priority. That wasn't entirely true. He sensed it since they crossed paths yesterday. Though he refused to look too closely at those feelings. Lewis stole a sidelong glance at her. "Just ask."

"What?"

Shit. All his plans for them to find that mushroom-shaped cottage in complete silence just flew the coop. Too late to take it back. He'd leaped off the cliff. Now he just had to go with it. "Whatever it is you want to know."

"What makes you think there's something I want to know?"

"I can see it in your face." Maybe she believed she hid it. If so, it wasn't very well. Then again, he'd gotten good at reading people. It kept him safe all these years.

"Oh." Her eyebrows squished together as she grimaced. As if she had to select her next words carefully. That whatever questions lingered between them might scare him off. He told her they didn't need to know anything regarding the other.

Despite the permission he gave her, nothing came at him. For the first time since they met, he actually wanted her to just let it all fly. Lewis dragged a hand through his hair, balling it up in his fist. Releasing the hold, he blew out a heavy breath. "Whatever it is… Just ask," he repeated. "It's fine. I promise."

Biting her lower lip, she dipped her chin. Still, she hesitated. Like she had to dip her toe in the water, testing the temperature. "How long have you been here?"

Funny. Of all the questions he expected, that wasn't one of them. "I don't know." Although it was the truth, it didn't seem sufficient. As if he could offer her a better explanation. "Time passes differently in Wonder. I've tried to count the days…" his words trailed off as the memory of his time in that dungeon threatened to bubble forth. Lewis beat it back, locking it down tight. There were some things he wouldn't share. "It's impossible to track."

"But it's been a long time," she said matter-of-factly. Her gaze lifted to him briefly and promptly returned to the scattered carpet of leaves as they trekked forward. "That isn't what you thought I'd ask, is it?"

It sure as hell wasn't. Given his admission, it made more sense she'd ask about that. More details. More information. How could he share any part of his past? What had happened when he'd first arrived? No. It was better left alone. He swallowed to wet his parched throat.

His silence must've supported whatever theories tumbled around in her head. Because she nodded. "It's okay. I mean… that's your business. Doesn't seem like my place to ask, but I'm a good listener… If you ever want to talk about it."

Lewis opened his mouth. *Fuck.* Was he actually going to share something? But the words just collected in the back of his throat. As if something blocked them from escaping.

"Hey." Alicia placed a hand on his forearm and squeezed it. "We're good. You don't have to tell me. I guess I just… I wanted to know more about you. It seemed like you knew him and I've never had anyone defend me like that."

He couldn't say what got him talking at that moment. The weight of her palm on his forearm, her tender touch, or the truth that sparkled in her eyes. "I was imprisoned. When I first arrived. And the queen… she enjoyed forcing me to fight her soldiers. As entertainment."

A small gasp left Alicia's mouth. Her eyes widened in abject horror. The grip she had on his arm tightened. "Good Lilith," she whispered. "I'm so sorry."

Lewis dropped his gaze, staring at the earth beneath their feet. The sun-dappled leaves that rolled across the thick strands of grass grounded him. Reminding him they weren't anywhere near those four walls. The queen had done so much worse to him. A shudder swept through him as the memories threatened to burst to the surface. He lifted his eyes, focusing on the bright-blue gaze meeting his. "Things got bad. I nearly died twice. After the last time, I knew that if I didn't escape… it would claim my life. I've been in hiding since, trying to find a way out of Wonder."

Her eyes held his. "I promise you, Lewis. They won't get you again. I won't let them. And we *will* get out of here… back to our world."

He believed her. It wasn't just the conviction in her words, but it was in the way she looked at him. Like she'd set the world on fire before letting any harm come his way. Along with something else he couldn't quite put his finger on. Compassion? Loyalty? Something more? Whatever it was, he wanted to drown in it. Feel every bit of what she offered. Lewis cupped her cheek. "Thank you." What the hell was he doing? *No!* She was a witch. Not to be trusted. Shaking off the force that drew them together, he cleared his throat and stepped back. "We should… uh… get moving."

Alicia visibly swallowed and a tight smile crossed her face. "Right." Turning away from him, she strode forward.

Whatever softness he saw dissipated. He watched as she walked away from him, moving deeper into the woods. *Shit.* The silence that stretched between them wasn't as awkward as it was during their travel through the underground tunnel system. Nope. Not awkward. It sizzled with something else entirely. Anger? Frustration? Disappointment? Or maybe all of it. This was what he got for opening up and letting her in. It was just a fraction, but he shouldn't have even done that. With a heavy sigh, Lewis traipsed after Alicia.

Damn Holloway. He never should've listened to that damn cat. If he hadn't, none of this would've happened. Instead of replaying his failure to keep her shut out, he focused on the spongy crunch of leaves under his boots. It's what he should've done to begin with. Finding some cottage tucked away in a thicket of trees was the first step toward their ultimate escape. Provided they could get out of here.

"I'm a pariah in my family," Alicia said. Her voice was so low he almost missed it. "Everything we do is supposed to be what's good for the faction. Follow a strict set of rules, live up to every expectation… never think of just yourself. Or what you want. Because it doesn't matter. We're only allowed to think of the whole, not the individual."

What could he say to that? Should he even say something? Of course, he should. They weren't supposed to be discovering anything about one another. Except every fiber in his being told him to offer comfort and encourage her to talk. It went against everything they agreed upon. But he should still say something. Where did he begin? Before he could find the right words, a cottage with a conical-shaped brown thatch came into view. The underside of the roof was a bright red. Lewis cocked an eyebrow at what sure as shit looked like a mushroom. "I think that's where we need to go."

"What makes you say that?"

"It matches the rumors." He'd never had a reason to find the blue worm, but that didn't mean he'd overlooked the grumblings. At least it had proven useful. Theoretically.

"So…" she peered over her shoulder at him as they both halted their steps. "Do we just knock?"

"It would be brusque to do otherwise," a deep, masculine voice commented behind them.

Lewis and Alicia both spun around at the sound. His hand immediately went to the hilt of his sword as he regarded the lean, dark-haired male who stood in front of them. Though Lewis didn't draw his weapon, he took a step forward, bettering his attack position and protecting Alicia at the same time. "Who are you?"

"The better question. *Who. Are. You?*" The male emphasized each word, drawing the last syllable out.

Could this be the one they were looking for? Given how the guy's appearance contrasted the greenery, it was highly probable. Who else would look like that? Standing there in a top hat, a pair of black trousers, a pale-blue vest, and a deep-blue jacket; the color reminded him of the night sky. While he needed to confirm this was the blue worm, he didn't want to ask outright. No one in the realm needed to know what they were up to. Lewis shot a look at Alicia, silencing her. Although her intervention worked with the twins, this time was different.

"Who. Are. You?" the male repeated, displeasure coating his tone.

How the fuck could they answer without providing an actual answer? His eyebrows drew together as he narrowed his gaze and discreetly unsheathed a portion of his blade. "We asked you first. It seems more prudent for you to answer before we do."

"As you are the interlopers, the opposite is true. Please, do put that matchstick away. Civility will get you further with me."

Interlopers? Matchstick? Christ, this male had a way with words. Though the guy hadn't directly come out with it, what he said confirmed his theory. This had to be the blue worm. And this was his home. Otherwise, the guy wouldn't have viewed them as intrusive. Releasing his hold of his sword's hilt, Lewis folded his arms across his chest and studied the male before them. "You don't look blue to me."

"And you don't look like a rabbit," the worm retorted. As he clasped his hands at the small of his back, he slowly encircled them.

A low growl left his mouth as he adjusted his stance, keeping Alicia behind him. He hated that fucking nickname. But he despised the way the worm walked around them, judgment clouding his face with every step. "If you know who we are, then why ask?"

"To see if you knew who you were."

"What kind of question is that? Of course, we do," Alicia blurted.

Damn it. Why the fuck couldn't she keep her mouth shut? The male didn't seem like a threat to them, but that didn't mean he wasn't. None of the rumors about the blue worm gave him any information regarding the male's powers. Whatever. If he had to shift to keep her safe, then he'd do that. Nothing would hurt her as long as he lived.

"Are you certain of that, witch?" The worm tilted its head. The pupil of its yellow eyes constricted, shifting from black to white. It shimmered, radiating like the color of the sun. "Your family has kept quite the secret. Fearful of your path, they hold you tight within their grasp. Shadows or light, no matter which you choose, you are destined for something new. Despite their efforts, the truth refuses to submit. Even now, it seeks you out. Determined to bring about a fate you cannot fight, no matter how hard you try."

"What the fuck?" Lewis uttered in a quiet breath. Maybe instead of trying to confirm the male's identity, he should've asked what the fuck he was. Because sure as shit, nothing about what just came out of the worm's mouth made a lick of sense. He glanced at Alicia. Her face blanched. Did she understand any of that?

The worm's gaze turned on Lewis. "Your past haunts you, day and night.

While you've tried to beat it back, her presence gives you nothing but pushback. You've seen that your fortunes are intertwined, though you refuse to accept what was designed. Fires will continue to grow within until you no longer know where she begins and you end. But that is not what you seek or what has led you to me. Find the golden brook and follow it to where spines hide in crooks. There you will find the heart of the matter, which has not yet shattered. But remember, you must follow the rules to release what you seek."

Before either of them could get on with a bunch of what-the-fucks, the worm disappeared in a cloud of smoke. It was almost like he witnessed one of those magic tricks performed on a New York stage. Just with a little less flare. Lewis stared at the empty spot, desperately trying to ignore part of what the worm had stated. His chest tightened as his stomach hardened. As much as he wished he didn't comprehend half of what the worm meant, he couldn't. *But you can ignore it.* That he could.

"So… that… um…"

"Yeah," he muttered. Gripping the back of his neck, Lewis faced Alicia and purposely kept his eyes on the ground. At the moment, he couldn't look at her. Not without seeing all the worm had pointed out. "I think I know where we'll find your… book."

"Oh?" she paused. "So, you, um, got something out of… all of that?"

"There's a creek about a mile to the east of here." At least he believed that was the right direction. Dropping his hands to his hips, Lewis peered across the vast greenery. The trees were too dense for him to spot it from their current location, but he caught the scent of wet earth on the breeze coming from the east. "The way the sun shines down on it lights it up, making it appear gold. It leads to Heart Tower, a monastery."

"*'Where spines hide in crooks,'*" Alicia repeated. "That makes sense. Alright. I guess… lead the way."

His gaze dropped to her. His mind flashed to the pallor color of her skin. The worm's words got to her. Some part of him yearned to reach out and caress her cheek, comfort her, but he forced his hand to stay put. "Are you okay? After…"

Her blonde brows lowered as her blue eyes fixated on him. "Do you want to talk about what he said?"

Yeah, he should've seen that coming at him. Their brief connection earlier didn't mean either of them intended to open up further. Nor did it set them up to get their talk on. "No."

"Then neither do I. So, let's just go."

Yep. Screw the fates. No fucking way was he destined for another witch. Even if everything inside of him screamed, *Alicia is different.* He couldn't get on board. The fates could shove that preordained shit up their ass. His mate wasn't a witch. He'd repeat that, however many times it took to convince himself it was the complete and utter truth.

"Are we going?"

Clearing his throat, Lewis nodded and started forward. It took every ounce of strength he had to tear his gaze away from her ethereal beauty. Not that it did a damn thing to help with her exquisite scent wafting into his nostrils. *Not mine.* Even as he replayed those two words on an endless loop, he believed them less and less.

Fuck.

He was so screwed.

CHAPTER *eight*

ALICIA SLOWED HER pace as they traveled close to the grassy banks edging the shallow water. The sun's rays lit the stream up, making it look like a river of gold. It was stunning to see. When she hadn't watched the water's natural ebb and flow, the blue worm's words danced on her brain. She tried not to give it too much thought but failed miserably. At least she hadn't paid attention to the quiet between her and Lewis as they made the trip. It gave her time to stew, her mind churning at what she knew of her family and questioning what she didn't.

It was one thing to recognize herself as an outsider, even in her own family, but for a stranger to emphasize those differences… especially with an unusual explanation. Or one that lacked clarity. What the hell could her family have hidden from her? She bumped right into Lewis, hitting his back as he came to an abrupt halt. Stumbling backward, she nearly fell on her ass. As she caught her footing, a deep frown settled across her face.

"What the…?" her words trailed off as she spotted the enormous cylindrical brick tower that loomed ahead. Her eyes widened as she drank it all in. A massive stone temple with several passages and hidden stairways rose from the ground like a hand, praising Lilith herself. Her gaze flipped from one spacious balcony to another, resting heartily between tall pillars. It was extraordinary. She'd seen nothing like it before.

"Yeah," Lewis murmured as one corner of his mouth lifted. Like he shared a secret with her.

Gods, however, would they find her family's grimoire in there? The place was fucking massive. Who knew the number of places it could've gotten hidden? Or what tests they might cross? Unless… "Have you been here before?"

"You could say that." He cocked an eyebrow at her. "Why do you ask?"

"I was thinking about the rules." And the confined spaces. Though if they had another moment like what they shared earlier, she wouldn't mind that. Alicia cast her eyes at him, studying his profile as he stared at the brick tower. His words hadn't been the only thing that had caught her off guard. She'd seen something unexpected in that golden-brown gaze of his— common ground. They both yearned for freedom from their gilded cages.

Earlier, it had only slightly bothered her that he'd backed off from her. She imagined he noted their equal desire, too. Possibly even felt it when his palm touched her face. But fear was one hell of a driver.

"Most of them are fairly simple. Keep your voice low and don't address the monks." His body angled toward her as he leaned in a little closer. "Can you tell if your book is in there?"

There was magic, but that didn't mean it belonged to the grimoire. Maybe she could sense it another way. Closing her eyes, Alicia shut everything out. She steadied her breathing, slowed her heart rate, and quieted her mind. The sound of trickling water softened, the wind sliding through blades of grass eased. Her surroundings all but disappeared.

With a shallow breath, she extended her senses, focusing solely on that slight hum beneath her skin. It writhed and rolled across the earth like the tendrils of a storm, touching everything within its reach. Inch by inch, it waded through the nooks and crevices of the monastery. It didn't stop until it hit a solid block. Her eyes popped open as she blew out a cold puff of air. "It's there. Third floor. Along the west wall."

"You can tell all of that?"

Alicia cracked a small smile. "With a little concentration, you'd be surprised at the details one can obtain." That was more than she expected to sense. Although she'd witnessed her grandmother discover more than that in the past, this particular trick never worked well for her. None of what she had in her arsenal usually did. All of which she kept to herself.

"At least it gives us our bearings. Depending on what it takes to get it off whatever shelf it's occupying, this should be a quick in and out."

Lilith, she prayed he didn't just jinx them.

His eyebrows furrowed, his honey-colored stare fixating on her. "Are you okay? You just went a little pale."

Not in the slightest. "I'm fine. Let's go get the grimoire." She refused to let her nerves get the best of her.

"If you say so." With a slight shake of his head, he started toward the back of the monastery. "This way, princess."

They were back to that shit again? Here she thought they'd gotten past all of that. What the fuck ever. Alicia bit her tongue as she followed him. Perhaps she needed to come up with a nickname for him. Sounded like an excellent idea. Jackass. Arrogant Prick. No. Both were far too subtle. She needed something that really stood out.

Nothing truly unique came to mind. Whatever. However long it took, she'd come up with something. They had other things to worry about right now. Trailing him, she eyed the high hedges they walked alongside. It seemed almost out of place for a monastery. Unless the intent was to hide the books inside the brick and mortar. That made no sense. Why would someone hide books?

As they rounded the corner, Lewis halted in his steps. He propped his hands on his hips. They stood there, side-by-side, staring across an exquisite garden. Flowering trees and bushes popped with color all around: reds, blues, oranges. A warm breeze stirred the blossoms, filling the air with a complex perfume of fresh and spicy. It stunned her into complete and utter silence.

"Whatever you do… don't let them pull you in." His words held a grim tone to them. Without extrapolating further, he strode forward.

As they walked, she eyed the various ornamentals. With the sun beating down on the back of her neck, she noted how droplets of dew slowly dried. The sound of their footsteps sank quietly into the damp earth. Despite the tranquility of all the colors, the surrounding silence grated on her. No insects hummed, not a single bird sang. Strange.

"You're beautiful."

Alicia blinked and shot a glimpse in Lewis' direction. "Did you say something?"

"No. Keep moving."

Her mind must be playing tricks on her. She could've sworn she'd heard something. Either that or she had lost it. This place could've affected her in ways neither of them considered.

"You smell quite delicious."

"Divine."

"Remarkable."

"So remarkable."

The voices were barely louder than a whisper. Yet they sounded so crisp.

"But not powerful enough."

"You'll never get free."

"We can help you."

"Make you strong."

"Come closer. Let us help you."

The words came out in a soft sing-song voice, overlapping one another and blurring together. Her steps slowed as her eyes fell on a vast rose bush. The open buds were almost life-size, standing close to her height. Their scent, oh gods, their heavenly aroma invaded her nostrils, consuming every part of her body. She took one step and then another, drifting toward them.

"Yes, come closer."

"We can help you."

"Touch us."

It seemed the most natural thing in the world to stretch her arm out, reaching for the brightly colored, silky petal—a thick hand grasped her wrist, jerking her backward. She was drawn roughly against a solid wall of male chest. Warmth spread through her, like a fire lighting her synapses up. It snapped her out of whatever had captivated her attention.

"What are you doing?" Lewis hollered. "I told you not to let them pull you in."

"Without us, you will fail," the roses hissed.

Alicia's eyes widened. "What the fuck?" Familiars talked, but not fucking plants. These things had teeth that snapped at her as if she were food. Impossible! Her gaze snapped to Lewis. "Christ! What the hell are those?"

"Capers. And they're poisonous. One touch of a thorn, you're out and meat for the grinding." His eyes locked on hers. "There's a reason I told you not to listen. Tune them out." He tugged her back several steps. "Come on. We're almost to the door."

Holy fuck. If he hadn't been so close, she could've… shit. Her breathing rasped as she struggled to control the tremors throughout her body. Lewis kept a firm hold on her arm and led her to the monastery's entrance. Alicia glanced over her shoulder, the roses disappearing from her sight as they moved along. Not that it eased the thoughts running rampant in her mind.

One touch would've knocked her on her ass. Out like fucking Sleeping Beauty or some shit. Her pulse raced and her heart pounded beneath her chest. Alicia jumped at the gentle click that went off.

"Hey. I got you," Lewis uttered. He nudged the door open further. Once they were inside, he drew her into his arms, enveloping her fully in his large body. "You're okay."

Squeezing her eyes shut, she crumpled against him. How could she have been so stupid? Regardless of their prior conversation, it truly hadn't occurred to her how little she knew of this world. So much could've gone awry if he hadn't been here or watched out for her. *Gods.* Tears speared the corners of her eyes and poured down her cheeks.

She couldn't say how long they stood like that. Pressed against the hard ridges of his chest with his strong protective arms clamped around her. Time stood still as his warmth eased the fear that had settled deep in her soul. It was like basking in the sun for hours. Alicia let out one last shuddering breath, wiped the tears from her face, and stepped out of his embrace. "Thank you."

Lewis cupped her jaw, brushing the wetness from her cheek. Those fierce golden-brown orbs of his captured her gaze. The look on his face softened. "I'll always keep you safe."

Her breath caught in her throat. Something in his words set her synapses ablaze. It wasn't so much as what he said, but the thickness in his voice. Unable to stop herself, she leaned into his lingering touch. The heat of his palm had her stomach fluttering. Really, they should get back to whatever they came here for, but she couldn't tear her eyes from his or force her feet to move.

A heady energy sizzled between them. One that she almost swore had a rich aroma. Lewis gently stroked his thumb across her lower lip. His gaze dropped from her eyes to her mouth. Clearing his throat, his hand fell to his side as he stepped back. Just like that, whatever connection existed broke. "We should, uh… we should… we should go."

All she could do was nod. No matter how much she tried to find her voice, it refused to function. Alicia swallowed hard. Did she actually *want* him to kiss her? Yes, she did. Funny. The last thing she expected was the way her chest constricted because he didn't do something. Shaking the sensation off, she studied the interior of the building.

Bright, clean white light filtered in through a host of windows. Torches lined the brick walls, adding to both the ambience and streaming luminescence. An innumerable amount of books, varying in color, rested on bookshelf upon bookshelf, discreetly built into the structure. A small gasp left her mouth as her eyes lifted higher and higher. "Good Lilith." There were so many.

"It's quite a sight," Lewis whispered.

Of that, they agreed. Her gaze landed on the spiral staircase to their right. Before he could stop her, she strode toward it and took the upward winding steps. The power that she sensed earlier from her family's grimoire called out to her. It was almost like an invisible tether dragging her closer to where the worn leather book sat.

Alicia passed by a wealth of hidden treasures. With her target locked, she didn't pay any attention to her steps and nearly plowed into someone in a dark-gray hooded robe. A hand came over her mouth. Lewis spun her around and pinned her against a cold stone wall. With his palm against the brick on one side of her head, he pressed a finger to his lips, silencing her as the monk waltzed by them. They seemingly went unnoticed.

Fuck! She bit back a groan. How could she forget? It slipped her mind that they had to avoid these fuckers. Although he hadn't elaborated what would happen if they ran into one, after the roses… it was better that she listened. As they remained interlocked in that position, her eyes traced the outline of his mouth. What would it be like to kiss those plump, pink lips? She could almost taste their richness.

A low rumble resounded in his chest. Her eyes snapped to his, locking on them like a missile. No way he knew the thoughts tumbling around her brain. But something raw burned in those golden-brown orbs. They darkened; the color a mix of deep amber and rich caramel. It was like staring at a hungry bear, ready to pounce on its next meal. Her. Heat pooled between her thighs. Shivers shot down her spine. Dear gods. He could eat her alive and she'd let him.

Lewis swallowed and shoved off the wall. Despite the distance he placed between them, the sparks still hovered. While they could ignore them for now, the thing about sparks… once they ignited, there was no stopping the fire. Eventually, it burned until something quenched it.

It was just a matter of time.

Neither of them spoke a word as she stepped forward. They had a grimoire to retrieve.

Carter stalked around the altar holding the still-beating heart she'd spelled last night. So much rode on their success and her knave had yet to report his findings. She paced in a continuous circle, the heels of her stilettos clicking against the glossy hardwood floor. The sound echoed around the empty chamber, like the reverberation of a bullet that ricocheted without finding its mark.

As she started another trip around the altar, she scowled at the beauty of the ballroom staring back at her. Its vaulted ceiling and hand-carved moldings were a stark contrast to the thick velvet drapery covering the three French doors. Massive tiered, crystal chandeliers hung overhead; their soft light glittering high above her. In all of their time here, she'd never once used this room. It served as nothing more than a reminder of all they'd lost.

The night their lives forever changed replayed in her mind.

"Carter Stone, I find you guilty of treason against your witch brethren. Do you have anything to say for yourself before sentencing?"

Her sister's nasally voice grated on her nerves. The words that left the bitch's mouth had her ears pounding. She clenched and unclenched her fists. With each move, the metallic cuffs tight around her wrists, preventing her use of magic, bit into her flesh. How in the fuck could they find her guilty? "I've done nothing wrong," Carter snapped. "None of what happened is my fault."

"Not your fault?" Helena's sapphire-blue eyes narrowed at her. "Three members of our faction are dead! We warned you incessantly that this kind of magic was dangerous. Forbidden! Not only did you choose to use it, you involved other witches. You and your bonded mate…" Her sister's mouth twisted in disgust. "Their blood is on your hands. The damage you've done is irreparable. Can you not even acknowledge that?"

No. She informed them how to protect themselves. If they'd followed her instructions, then none of this would've happened. Those idiots died because they hadn't heeded her words. They all thought they knew better, that they could outperform her. Their arrogance led to their demise. Carter sneered. "My only regret is that I didn't kill them myself."

Helena's lips pressed tightly into a grimace. Taking in a slow breath, her gaze focused on Carter. "So be it," her sister replied. "Carter Stone, you shall be imprisoned for all of eternity. Never to walk the earth. Nor feel the breeze upon your skin. You shall never know what has become of your line. Nor will you carry power again of your own."

"No! You can't do this!" Imprisonment? No magic? Impossible!

Ignoring her outburst, Helena peered at someone behind Carter. Whoever they were, they stood outside of her line of sight. "Have they agreed?" her sister posed. The pounding in Carter's ears had gotten so loud she couldn't hear their response. Her sister nodded. Whatever reply they delivered didn't favor either her or Jaq.

"Very well," her sister continued. "I sentence you and your mate to a bond of death. One that will cease the aging process. You shall bear no children. Know no love or warmth. No matter how much the two of you are together, you will forever remain apart."

A pair of firm hands grabbed her arms. Carter fought, writhing against the hold. "No! You can't do this! There must be balance!" It was the only thing she had going for her. A spell that potent demanded balance. A means of escape. "There must!"

"Oh, there is." A slow, sadistic smile crossed her sister's face, twisting the female's lovely features into something sinister. "Only a bond more remarkable than yours can set you free. And we'll never let that happen."

"No!" Carter screamed as they dragged her away.

Her faction made this a prison. It had taken a millennium to free herself from the cuffs. Longer to regain even the smallest amount of magic. All of which she stole from others. Her power was nothing like it used to be. Not that it stopped them. Together, she and Jaq turned things around.

At least in a sense. They felt nothing. Not love or warmth. Not joy or passion. But they turned that to their advantage. Pain became pleasure. Fear became a tool. Every step, every plan they made… it all served one purpose: revenge. She didn't know how much time had passed in the real world. It wouldn't stop them from finding and killing every living member of her faction and his pack.

Both were equally responsible for their suffering.

Her brows furrowed as she realized she'd stopped her endless loop around the altar. Carter strolled across the ballroom to the closest set of French doors. Taking the soft fabric in her hands, she yanked the drapes apart and threw open the doors. She eyed the elegant floral arrangement dotting the stone terrace. Vibrant blooms of every hue danced in the sunlight; their sweet fragrance carried on the gentle breeze. Its beauty was out of place with all the nothingness she felt.

A pair of soft-soled boots resounded as Jaq approached. She knew the sound of his strides anywhere. "It's done," he called out. "They're on their way to the grimoire."

"Good." Despite the word, her tone remained utterly flat. They were so close to tasting freedom and she couldn't even enjoy it. "Everything else is in place?"

"Yes. The guards have their orders. They should take care of it."

Carter peered over her shoulder at him. Regardless of his affirmation, he sounded… hesitant. Unsure. Of course, he had a question. They had spent years together and he still didn't trust her. "What?"

"Are you sure this is the right couple? That they'll bond?"

No. She wasn't certain of anything except what they required. They'd searched for eons for these two, getting the egg delivered from one person to another. All through dreams. Even once they had Lewis in their grasp, he was only half of the equation. They'd imprisoned, abused, and tortured him, doing whatever it took to summon his other half. That still took twenty years. With all that, she only had one answer. "They must."

"And if they don't?"

"Then we will wait until they do." Facing the terrace, she stared at the bright-blue sky. The sun wouldn't dip below the horizon for a few more hours. Waiting had never been her strong suit, but waiting was all they had.

CHAPTER
nine

LEWIS STOPPED AT the edge of the forest, taking one last glimpse at Heart Tower. It was aptly named. The place stirred something inside of him. Something he didn't want. No matter what parts of his anatomy it awakened, he had to nip this shit before it burrowed so deeply that he couldn't stop it. He surveyed the horizon, ensuring nothing followed them, and then eyed the path forward.

Starting forward, he glanced at Alicia out of his periphery. "We've got a long trip ahead of us. Be mindful of your surroundings. There is almost always something out there ready to attack." Sure as fuck, he didn't need to hold her again. *Yes, you do.* No, the fuck he didn't. Yeah, it felt damn good to have her in his arms. He couldn't get accustomed to it. They'd already agreed to go their separate ways once they escaped.

"I got it. Trust me, I've learned my lesson."

Fuck, he hoped so. His heart palpitated the closer her hand got to those roses' teeth. Nothing had ever terrified him so much as in those seconds. At least they were heading away from them. They hadn't gone too far into the forest. Still. No chance they'd have a repeat of that problem. "I'm not so sure about that. Honestly, after the fire situation and the garden, I think you have a death wish."

Her head swiveled in his direction. "Excuse me?" Alicia's jaw clenched as she glowered at him. "I screwed up, but that doesn't mean I'm trying to get myself killed."

Folding his arms across his chest, he cocked an eyebrow at her. It'd occurred far too many times for his liking. It led to desires that shouldn't have found their way into his heart. Her continual defiance drove him crazy. If, for once, she listened to him, then he wouldn't have this incessant need to taste her. To have her. To own every part of her body.

It occurred to him they'd stopped walking. His ears twitched. The wind rustled a cache of leaves. The snap of a twig underfoot caught his attention. Lewis lifted his nose and took a deep whiff of the air. The stale scent of must filled his nostrils, overriding the sweeter smells of earth in this part of Fogley Forest.

They weren't alone.

"Run," he whispered.

"What?"

"Run." No time to explain. Thankfully, Alicia didn't seem to require it. She darted between the tall trees, taking off into the forest with brief hesitation. Not that he had a fucking clue where they could go. It would be open season on them if the guards caught up with them. *Shit.* He should've thought about this, considered a place for hiding. Except no way those soldiers figured out which direction they disappeared. Unless the fuckers found a witness. Not a rebel. A supporter of the Red Queen.

They couldn't outrun the queen's guard. Something else he should've thought about. They needed some place to hide. There wasn't anywhere in the immediate vicinity. Shit. *Think.* Where could they… a cabin flashed in his mind. Right. It sat buried in the depths of the forest. And it would keep them hidden. Provided they could find the path.

One problem at a time.

If nothing else, at least he had a general idea of its location. It'd concealed him from prying eyes once before. Racing alongside Alicia, he grabbed her hand and drew her toward the east. "This way." Even with as fast as they ran, their feet pounding hard against the ground, the soldiers would eventually catch up with them. Fuck. They could move faster if he shifted and she rode atop him, but there wasn't time for them to make that switch. Another thing he hadn't—

A sharp, burning sensation lanced his left shoulder. Throwing his balance off, he threw out a hand and caught himself before he fell to his knees. The bark scratched his flesh as his palm connected with the trunk, setting his pain receptors off all over again. His gaze dropped to where he held Alicia's hand within his own. At least he had the good sense to let go. Otherwise, he could've taken her down with him. Not that he hit the ground. As blood bloomed across the cotton fabric of his shirt, he spotted the head of the copper-coated arrow protruding from his body. *Motherfucker.* Here, he thought, they just wanted to capture him.

Nope. They were out to kill him.

"Why did you—? Oh, my god!" Alicia's brows shot up, her eyes latching onto the arrow that pierced his shoulder. She reached out for the shaft.

"Don't touch it." While he didn't think it could hurt her, he wouldn't chance it. Voices erupted throughout the forest behind them. Lewis glanced over his shoulder. The armed guards were far too close for his liking. "Come on. We need to keep moving." Regardless of what they planned for him, he wouldn't let them get near Alicia.

"We can't leave that in there."

"And we can't linger." His eyes locked on hers. They couldn't deal with it where they stood. Not that he was certain how far he'd make it. He'd take her as far as he could. While he didn't give a shit about himself, he'd fight with his dying breath to keep her alive.

Alicia grunted under Lewis' heft as they repositioned him for the third time. She didn't know how far they'd traveled since he got hit. The distance mattered little in the scheme of it all. What she cared about were the voices and hammering footsteps that got closer with every step they took. At this rate, they'd never escape the soldiers gunning after them.

"I need to rest," he said through gritted teeth. Beads of sweat rolled down his face as she propped him against a nearby tree. His complexion had paled even more than when they'd started down this path. His jaw clenched as he struggled to catch his breath.

She eyed the large crimson stain across his white tunic, noting how it had spread. Shit. Was he bleeding out? Had the arrow nicked an artery or something? Or was there another issue altogether? Either way, he'd never make it.

"You need to go on without me," Lewis stated as if she uttered her thoughts aloud.

"Have you lost your fucking mind? I'm not leaving you." Didn't they already establish that? Fuck, he looked like hell.

"Then we'll both die." A pained expression crossed his face as he stared at her. "I won't let that happen to you. Just take the mushrooms out of my pouch and find the path."

"No." Alicia scoured the treeline, scanning for the guards that raced in their direction. There were far too many to take on. Not without jeopardizing Lewis' life and her own. There was only one way for them to get out of this.

To survive.

Shutting out the sound of nature, she fixed her eyes on him. "Focus on me." She needed to get him out of his head, thinking about anything other than the pain. Strengthen their connection.

"Just. Go," he said between breaths.

Fuck. He needed to focus on her, not on the pain. Repeating her request was useless. Only one thought came to mind. It was a stupid idea, but what else did she have? They couldn't get caught. Not now.

Alicia wrapped a hand around the back of his neck. She stroked her thumb up and down his nape, pushed up on her tiptoes, and pressed her lips to his. *Oh gods!* His lips were soft. A complete contrast to his ruggedness. He was like a heady wine on her tongue. She could easily get drunk off of him.

He grabbed her by the waist and crushed her body to his. A searing heat blazed between them as a small, breathless moan escaped her lips. His tongue swept along the seam of her mouth, demanding more. Without a second thought, she opened for him. Their tongues danced as each of their bodies melted together, disappearing from the world, blending as if they were one with the tree.

While she'd kissed him to get his mind off of the pain radiating through him, it went beyond that. That current she felt anytime their eyes connected thrummed in her very soul. Power, unlike anything she ever held before, surged through her. It remained steadfast, even as their lips parted and the kiss ended. They both let out slow, shallow breaths as their eyes locked on one another. Hunger and concern glazed his golden-brown orbs. Although she'd happily respond to both, this wasn't the time or place.

Holding his gaze, she pressed a slender finger to her mouth. Blessed silence stretched between them. As long as they stayed still and their respiration rate didn't change, no one would find them.

"Where the hell did they go?"

A male marched forward, stopping a few feet from where they hid. He turned in their direction and looked right over them, as if he saw nothing more than the large oak tree. "I don't know, but it couldn't have been far."

"Keep searching. Find them. They have to be here somewhere."

Minutes ticked by as they held true to their position. The soldiers darted off in various directions, searching the greenery and shrubs for them. Once the footfalls of the untold numbers of guards faded, she stepped out of Lewis' hard body and offered him her hand. "Let's move," Alicia whispered.

"What did you do?"

"Invisibility spell." The two words were simpler than the concentration it actually required. It wasn't complex by any means. Nor did it require any words. One of the more useful spells in her repertoire. Considering they were still being hunted, it made sense to keep it up. At least until they got somewhere safe.

"You could've left me," he mumbled, pushing away from the trunk. His heavy arm draped across her shoulders as she wrapped an arm around his waist.

"I told you I'd never do that. Now, how far away is this cabin? I'm worried that the arrow hit an artery." Though if it struck anything vital, he wouldn't be upright and walking. It had damaged something. Otherwise, it wouldn't have this kind of effect on him.

"Not sure. Only been there once." With a slight huff, he dug into the pouch at his side and retrieved two mushroom caps similar to the ones they ate yesterday. "These should show us the way."

"Will we see lights again?" This was becoming a thing. Alicia popped one into her mouth as he chewed on the other.

"Yeah," he replied around the shroom. They limped along, leaves quietly crunching under their feet with every staggering step they took. The surrounding stillness was more comfortable than it had been between them. "Can I ask you something?"

"Shoot."

When she didn't immediately get anything back, she figured he reconsidered whatever bounced around his head. He blew out a soft breath. "Why'd you kiss me?"

Fuck. It wasn't a question she expected, yet she should have. The few shared moments didn't warrant a kiss, considering the timing. Initially, it had been about calming him and getting him to focus on her. Information she was hesitant to share. Since something else transpired when it happened. Could she address both? Give him some explanation that held the true depth of what she felt at that moment?

"It's okay. You don't have to answer."

Her reticence said too much and nothing at all. Her eyebrows furrowed as she smirked. "It's complicated. I'm trying to understand it myself. Why I started it isn't how it ended." Did that help? Probably not. Surely, he needed something more. While she tried to find the right words, she spotted a pale, glowing light embedded in a path just up ahead. "Is that what we're looking for?"

"That's it."

At least one thing was going for them. As they followed the line of luminescence with careful steps, she monitored his respiration and heart rate. They stopped as often as he required. Though she wanted to remove the shaft from his shoulder, it made more sense to wait until they arrived at their destination. The only sounds she heard along their trip, aside from their shuffling feet, were the scrabbling claws of small animals and the delicate breeze swaying through the trees.

In hindsight, the peaceful trek should've warned her of the shock that was about to drop in her lap. Not that it changed a thing.

A few yards in front of them, a large log cabin sat nestled in a thicket of trees. The grove looked as if it attempted to reclaim parts of the land. Despite the long grass and wildflowers growing around the cabin, it appeared freshly built or well-tended. Rays of the sun reflected off the clean windows, making them shine ever so slightly. "Uh, let's get you inside."

"Looks like I remember."

"Really? How long ago were you here last?" If it had been a matter of months, that made sense. If more time had passed, then how the fuck wasn't this place dilapidated?

With a shrug, Lewis winced. "Not sure. A while ago."

Right. Just one more thing to add to the growing pile of *that made no sense.* Together, they made their way up the short flight of stairs. She released her hold on him long enough to open the door and scrutinize the cabin's interior. A kerosene lantern hung next to the doorjamb. In the living room sat a long, strong-backed couch, a small wooden coffee table, and a tall fireplace. There was a twin-sized bed against the right wall. The back of the cabin contained a small kitchen with a wood-burning stove. Nothing really stood out, except it was clean and devoid of holes.

Stepping aside, she opened the door further and gave him plenty of berth to enter. Once he was inside, she shut them in together. "Sit on the couch and take your shirt off while I see if I can find some supplies to clean that wound."

"I'll do what I can."

Where the arrow had struck, it wouldn't surprise her if he needed help. Alicia scoured every cabinet in the kitchen and the bathroom she located. The place had various food items, utensils, plates, and other sundry. But not much in the way of first aid. Just some dry linens, a needle, and thread. She'd make it work. Returning to Lewis, she set the items on the wooden table and shucked her cloak.

"Sorry," he stated gruffly. "I didn't get far."

"That's okay." Alicia stepped in front of him and gently tugged the cotton material to the side. Green veins in a web-like pattern sprouting from the injury came into view, halting her hands. She gasped. Her eyes widened, snapping to his. Holy shit. "You're a shifter."

The words came out of their own volition. Not that she could've stopped them even if she tried. Her fingers lingered on the soft material of his tunic. Like they patiently waited for him to reject the declaration. Except he couldn't. The truth stared her in the fucking face. Explained why the injury affected him as it had. Those soldiers… they used a copper-lined head.

"Does this change things? Now that you know what I am?"

No. What she didn't understand… why didn't he simply tell her the truth? Except… shit. Her eyes narrowed at him. "You don't have any antivenin, do you?"

"No. And I'm not positive this place has the ingredients to make it."

"You knew," she said in a hushed tone. "That's why you told me to leave you." Alicia swallowed the lump in the back of her throat. If she did nothing, he'd die. Packing and sewing up the wound wouldn't do shit. Shifters healed on their own, but no way he came back from this. Unless… her eyes drifted shut. It wasn't something she'd ever attempted. What if she failed?

"Yes." The rough back of his knuckles brushed against her cheek. "I was slowing you down. Protecting you is my only priority."

Alicia set her gaze on him. Captured by the strength in that liquid-gold stare of his, failure was impossible. The power surging through her wouldn't buckle. "Do you trust me?"

Their eye contact never wavered. Nor did his touch leave her face. "Yes," he replied in a firm voice.

Her hold on his tunic tightened. "Then I'm going to save you." She spoke no truer words. And she knew she would.

Lewis watched as Alicia moved about the kitchen, mixing a salve to apply to his wound. His earlier agreement came out of him so easily. It threw him completely off guard. Nearly as much as her capabilities. She'd done exactly as she said and used her magic to draw the poison out of his body.

The relief that washed over him was like sunshine pouring into his very essence. His hands trembled as he slumped on the couch, heat radiating through his chest. Every part of him felt light, like nothing he'd ever experienced. Those sensations remained with him, even now.

He had no clue what to do with them.

Or her.

Alicia wasn't like the Red Queen. Alicia reminded him of a radiant light standing stark against the darkness. A warmth that suffused his icy heart. The more he saw, the more he got to know her, the more of her he wanted for himself. Leaving the kitchen, the female appeared at the end of the sofa as if summoned by his thoughts.

She stood there, her delicate fingers cradling a yellowed bowl in her hands. Her blue-sapphire eyes sparkled as a small smile touched the edges of her mouth. "What?"

"Nothing." He shook his head. Despite all she'd done for him, he swallowed the admission that sat poised on the tip of his tongue.

"Okay." Alicia sat beside him, tucking one leg under the other. She dipped her fingers into the mixture. "This might be a little cold, but it'll speed up your recovery." Lifting her hand, she gently smoothed the brown concoction over the line of black stitches. Something else she'd done with great precision.

"It's fine." It may have been cool, but if it was, he didn't notice it. He felt nothing but warmth as she caked the shit on.

As she brought up another scoop of the gook and spread it across his wound, her bright-blue eyes locked on his face. "The kiss. I never answered you earlier."

No, she hadn't. He hadn't expected more than what she'd previously given him. That maybe the flush of heat had only been on his side of things. Was he wrong? She bit her bottom lip. A low rumble percolated in his chest. Gods, he could fucking taste her as if they were kissing again. She hadn't even explained further. The waiting nearly killed him, but he wouldn't push her. Though the way her eyes shined and how she leaned in closer said it all. Didn't it?

Her eyes met his stare as a touch of pink tinged her high cheeks. "It started as a distraction… from your pain. But it changed. I wanted it. Needed it. Like oxygen in my lungs." The more she spoke, the huskier her words became.

Holy fuck. As he let out a deep growl, a breathless whisper escaped her mouth. Her sapphire blues didn't just gloss with need. Her rich, woodsy scent thickened with arousal. He'd held back once before, but he didn't know then how she tasted. That small sample wasn't enough. He wanted more. And not just her mouth. "If you keep looking at me like that, I can't help what happens next." He lost all resemblance of control. Unless she told him no or to stop. That was the only way to override the need driving him to take her.

Lifting her head high, her hooded gaze held onto his. "I'm not stopping you."

One word popped into his mind as he surged forward.

Mate.

CHAPTER
Ten

ALICIA'S HAND STILLED. Had those words come out of her mouth? Was that her voice? Yes, on both accounts. And she meant every single word. She allowed her eyes to drift lower, drinking in the deliciously exposed broad expanse of his chest. Her tongue snaked out across her bottom lip.

As if they came to some sort of accord, Lewis took the bowl from her hand, set it on the table, and all but launched at her. Like a torpedo on a mission, their mouths crashed against one another. Laying her back against the soft cushions, he kissed her, his tongue dipping in.

Her legs settled on either side of his body. As he nestled between her thighs, she let out a throaty sigh. She marveled at the breadth of his shoulders, her palms skimming his satin-smooth skin. The hard planes of his chest brushed against her breasts, sending a jolt through her. With a moan, Alicia deepened the kiss.

As if that was all the encouragement he required, Lewis fisted a handful of her hair. His deft fingers glided down her side, setting off another round of fireworks. Fuck. He'd hardly touched her and every bit felt amazing. Although she noted exactly how his weight settled against her, their bodies molded perfectly to one another.

Despite the raw hunger she saw on his face before he took her down on the couch, there was no urgency in the kiss. It remained slow and languid. They took their time teasing and tasting one another. Their tongues connected over and over as she ran her fingertips up and down the rippling muscles of his back.

As much as she enjoyed the warmth of his flesh under her hands, she longed to feel more of him. They hadn't even gotten to that thick length in his pants and she quivered with desire she'd never felt before. Begging for more, Alicia hooked a leg over his hip.

Lewis growled. Heat bloomed in the apex of her thighs. *Holy shit.* Nothing had ever sounded so fucking erotic. He wasn't anything like the lovers she had in the past. Not just the noises he made, but the power in his body. He had far more brawn than the warlocks she dated. With a few exceptions, most of them were sinewy and lean.

That only accounted for their physicality.

None of them had ever made her feel… safe. Shielded from the darkness. Certainly not like Lewis did. That just made her want him more. With nothing separating them. Skin on skin. As if he read her mind, he wrapped an arm around her back and slid a hand between them. His nimble fingers worked the ties of her corset. Breaking the kiss off, he trailed his lips down her jawline.

A faint grunt and tug of the cord that laced her corset drew her gaze to the top of his head. For a moment, she considered offering him aid, but before the words came out, Lewis freed the leather that bound her abdomen. "Fuck," he groaned as he gently pressed his hand against her stomach.

Fuck was right. Even through the thin cotton material of her blouse, she could feel the warmth and power radiating from him. Alicia arched her back, pushing her breasts against his chest.

"Gods," Lewis groaned. "Let me see you. I need you out of this. Now."

His gruff demand cranked the heat in her body up a notch. He hadn't even gotten her naked and she was so fucking turned on. It shouldn't be possible. Yet she was proof that it was. Propped up on an elbow and with some well-constructed shimmying, Alicia slipped the straps of the corset free from her shoulders. The peasant top came next, swept over her head, and tossed somewhere to the side. As she bared her breasts to him, a lovely sound vibrated in his chest.

Palming her bosom, he teased the tight, rosy bud of her nipple between his fingers. His head dropped low to the valley between her breasts. Their eyes met as the tip of his pink tongue stroked that heaving part of her flesh. Raw hunger crossed his dark, brooding features. The way his caramel eyes fixated on her, he looked practically starved and she was the only thing that could satiate him.

Without taking his eyes from hers, he captured the taut pebble of her other breast between his lips, sucking and lashing at her with his tongue. "Fuck." She raked her hand through his silky brown hair, gripping the back of his head. The carnality of the way he teased and taunted her drove her insane. Every time he brought her to the edge, he slowed down. Just to do it all over again.

Letting out a rumble of approval, he prowled down the length of her body, his mouth skimming across her abdomen. His darkened gaze glistened with desire. "I need to see all of you," Lewis said as he eased into a sitting position. He gripped the bottom of her boot and removed it with incredible finesse. Her other one followed suit. His eyes dropped to her leathers as if he requested permission to take them off.

Fuck. He had her panting, aching for a release. As juiced up as she was, she didn't quite trust her voice. Her words might come out shaky. There was no confusion about what she wanted on her part. Instead of a verbal response, Alicia undid the buttons and lifted her hips.

Covering her hands with his, he took over. Their eyes held onto one another as he jerked her pants and undergarments down her long legs. Once they were off, they flew over his shoulder and fluttered to the floor. Not that he'd focused anywhere but on her face. At least not until she bit her bottom lip. Lewis growled, his upper lip curling off the tip of one of his fangs.

That looked sexy as all hell.

His eyes raked over her, going lower and lower. The moment he saw her slit, a soft hiss escaped his mouth. His gaze shot back to her face. "You're bare," he said in a breathless whisper.

Alicia merely nodded. Although nothing in his tone gave her the impression this was a bad thing, she didn't know what to say. It had been like that her whole life. Unlike other witches, she only grew hair on her head. Just something else that made her… different.

Lewis stroked his thumb and forefinger along the outer edge of his mouth. "Fuck. I just need a taste." His hand moved to the soft skin of her inner thigh. Lowering his body, his shoulders bunched between her legs and his tongue swept up the moist warm folds between her thighs.

"Fuck," Alicia cried out as a burst of pleasure thundered through her. He'd gotten her so primed, she orgasmed from the small contact with no chance at stopping the avalanche. That seemed to be exactly what he wanted as he lapped at everything she gave him. He helped her ride the crest, driving his tongue into her until she peaked again.

When it finished, his head lifted. His tongue snaked out across slick and reddened lips. "Do you want to know what you taste like?" His long finger swept over her swollen cleft, drawing a moan out of her.

"Yes," she panted. With the way he stared at her, fiery need blazing in his eyes, she would've agreed to anything he asked.

"Like honey." He sucked the remnants of her juices from his fingers. "Sweet, succulent honey. And I love honey." His expression told her he planned to come back at her, but right then, he seemed hungry for something more. Standing, Lewis kicked off his boots and shucked his leathers. His erection stood straight out, pointing at her like a divining rod. And she was the only thing that could quench his thirst.

The sight of that thick, swollen masterpiece nearly sent her over the edge. Holy shit. She'd never seen a more beautiful male. Even with the dried salve spread over his wound and bits of it caked in his hair, he was utter perfection. Sculpted like a bronze statue. A combination of hard ridges and valleys. Made just for her.

Coming back down to the couch, he roamed up her body, hovering and settling between her thighs, fitting just as perfectly as he had for the first time. Their mouths fused together. Wrapping her arms around his shoulders, being careful of his injury, she dragged her nails over the contours of his back.

Lewis slipped an arm around her waist as she hooked her legs over his hips. Without thinking, she lifted her ass. The blunt head of his cock pressed against her entrance. He swung his hips, pumping back and forth, his hot shaft inching deeper inside of her with every stroke. Growing increasingly impatient, Alicia tightened her grip on his hipbone, dug her heels into his ass, and in one thrust, his shaft filled her to the hilt. They both groaned as his girth stretched her wide.

Then he moved, retracting and burying that hot flesh of his over and over, taking her back to that high. It was just as unhurried as the initial kissing. A slow discovery of what made her breathless and aching for a release. Until the passion became uncontrollable.

Breaking the kiss, he sat up ever so slightly and gripped her thighs, his fingers digging into the curve of her ass cheeks. With no regard, Lewis drove into her, hard and fast. Sweat bloomed on his forehead, trickling down his face, his muscles straining with each thrust. Her hips lifted, keeping to the incredible rhythm until, simultaneously, they flew apart.

They cried out in ecstasy at the primal pleasure that pulsed through them. Hot jets shot into her core, setting off her own orgasm in what seemed to have no end. Their ragged breathing was the only sound that filled the room for several moments as their mutual high waned.

"Are you okay?" she asked between heavy breaths.

"Yeah… I'm…" A broad grin spread across his face, lighting up his eyes, making them look more like a gemstone than cooked sugar. "You?"

Gazing into those golden orbs, for the first time in her life, she felt… alive.

Free. From her family and their expectations. As if she was more than a commodity.

Free to choose her own path.

To be herself.

"More than okay." Because she couldn't imagine anything better than this moment with him.

"Good."

Mesmerized by the slight glow of his eyes, she almost missed the way his rigid length still filled her. Their bodies remained locked onto one another. "You're still hard."

"Yes, I am."

"You gonna do something about it?" Alicia gyrated her hips, contracting her sex around his shaft, ensuring he got the picture.

"Abso-fucking-lutely," he growled. "I'm nowhere near done. Far from it."

Words that almost sent her back over that glorious edge. They dripped with everything they had to look forward to. And nothing of what waited for them on the other side.

Carter glowered at the male in front of her. Another soldier explained how they once again lost the trail of the witch and rabbit. Two mongrels that shouldn't be this difficult to track. They couldn't offer any information whether that damn shifter survived his injury. It was all too fucking important that he did. Especially if those two hadn't yet fully bonded. It was on the tip of her tongue to scream, *Off with his head!*

Perhaps the loss of another guard would rectify their incompetence. Her long fingernails drummed against her throne's upholstery. Static prickled her skin, awakening her senses. What the hell? Sitting up a little straighter, she scrutinized her second-in-command.

His gaze met hers for a moment as he rolled his neck. He clenched and released his fingers, cranking them into fists.

Was it just them? Were they the only ones who noticed the shift that thrummed about the atmosphere? Her heart thundered behind her ribcage as she refocused on those gathered below, studying the blank expressions on each of their faces. Nothing about them stood out. They all merely appeared as if they all eagerly awaited her response.

Did that mean…

Had it happened?

There was only one way to tell.

Inhaling and exhaling, she concentrated on the sensations flooding her body. Jolts of lightning shot through her, a storm brewing beneath her flesh. Her eyes widened as she lifted her palm, red sparks dancing across her fingers, licking at the blackened nail beds. Crazed by the long-forgotten power that surged through her, she stretched out her hand, reaching toward the incompetent messenger. "Off with his head." A burst of red energy shot out, whooshed through the air, and sliced the guard's neck. His body crumpled as his head fell, rolling across the marble floor.

Carter cackled in sheer delight. Warmth radiated throughout her body, her heart racing in her chest. This had to be what people boasted regarding joy. For the first time in millennia, she felt like a young witch eagerly awaiting their full power. It wouldn't all return at once, but those two had begun the bonding process. By the end, every ounce of magic her sister stole from her would be back in full force.

Now, she simply had to ensure they held to their course. Steepling her fingers, she regarded the crowd of soldiers. Despite her little demonstration, their panic-riddled eyes remained forward, focusing on her rather than the dead male on the ground. Good. As much as she'd enjoy punishing others, she needed her full strength for their escape. "Failure is *not* an option. What are you waiting for? Find them!" she barked.

"You heard your queen," the knave tacked on as the group ran out of the throne room, tripping over themselves to get away from the gruesome display pooling onto that shiny surface beneath their feet.

Neither of them said anything more until all the guards left, save for those posted around the room. Carter stood. "Did you feel it?"

"A slight shift?" Jaq clasped his hands at the small of his back, scanning the empty building for non-existent threats.

Not that he'd find anything. Nothing overshadowed the control they claimed all those years ago. After they departed, well, that would be up to the idiots of Wonder to replace them. Unless the magic that created this place disappeared afterward. Wouldn't that be a shame? The corners of her mouth upturned into a wicked grin. "Yes." Her eyes dropped to the goosebumps lining her flesh. "I believe it's high time we offer a proper celebration to the good people of Wonder. We have that second ballroom."

"Do you think that's wise? With what we have in the works."

"All the more reason to host something. Shining a light on the path would be far too obvious, but we can illuminate the sky, so they find us." They couldn't know the part they played in everything. Though with her sister's proclamation, she imagined much was kept under wraps. Still, with a bonded witch almost within her grasp, she needed to minimize every risk possible. All without leading the damn female to do exactly as the spell demanded.

"A distraction for the people and a beacon for our guests of honor."

"Exactly." But when? How much time did they give the rabbit and his conquest? Carter raised her hand and summoned her magic, the delicate push and pull of red energy undulating across her palm. "Send the ravens out. Set it for two days' time." If they got too close before then, the soldiers could slow them down. So everything played out to her desire.

Because sometimes you had to sacrifice pawns to win the war.

CHAPTER *eleven*

LEWIS GINGERLY RAN his fingers up and down Alicia's outer upper arm. He traced over the invisible lines of her smooth skin. Over the last few hours, they made their way to the bed. At least, what constituted a bed. It wasn't anything more than a mattress atop a wooden frame, covered in a thin layer of sheets, and a single duvet. With their sheen of sweat, they kept each other warm enough. That wouldn't last, though. Especially as the sun dipped below the horizon.

There was a handful of logs beside the hearth. He could get a fire going when the time came. They'd need more to get them through the night. Along with food. Something they'd resolve soon enough. Out of his periphery, he watched the gentle rise and fall of Alicia's chest. Her breaths coming out in a steady rhythm.

He'd never connected with someone so well before. Not even his pack. But that was how it was supposed to be with mates, from what he heard. It was still strange that Alicia could be that for him. She was a witch.

The enemy.

Whom he had the urge to protect from the beginning. A feeling the mind-blowing sex only strengthened. Which maddened him. They didn't even know one another. Not in the depth that he knew his brothers. His pack. Despite the time apart, that went unchanged. Yet he'd fight with the same energy and prowess for her as he would for them. No, that wasn't right. For her, he'd do more. Go further. Fight harder. He'd die for her.

"What are you thinking about?" she murmured against his pec.

"Nothing. And everything."

"That's vague." Repositioning, Alicia rested her chin on her hand and stared up at him. "Are you sure it's not about how many orgasms we just experienced? Because I didn't know it was physically possible to have that many."

He chuckled. That might've crossed his mind, but wasn't a prominent feature of his forethoughts. "Oh, I'm sure if we tried, we'd find a few more in there."

"Seems a little excessive." Her blue gaze narrowed as a smirk settled across her features, challenging him, daring him to counter her statement.

"Not in the least." Turning onto his side, Lewis wrapped an arm around her narrow waist and crushed her body to his. He brushed a soft kiss across her lips. Her scent thickened, a sweet and spicy aroma filling his nostrils. "I can smell the way you're opening up for me. The heat rushing through you. Ready to accept my body." Gods, it was like she was his fucking drug of choice. The more of her arousal he caught, the more his body stirred. His sex thickened and lengthened, pressing against her thigh. "And it's getting my cock hard." This wasn't the direction he'd seen this conversation taking, but the second she mentioned sex, he popped an erection. It was like he was a teenager all over again.

Alicia nipped his ear and whispered, "I can tell." Her nails skated across his thick, muscular shoulders, trailing down his spine, inching lower and lower. Her palms slid over his ass, giving it a hard squeeze.

"You must like me out of control," he growled. If she kept this up, he'd lose it all over again. Snap like a broken rubber band. Rolling her beneath him, he gripped her wrists, lifted them above her head, and pressed them down into the mattress.

"Maybe." A small breathless whisper escaped her lips as she arched her back, undulating underneath him. Her nipples felt like little pebbles against his chest.

Staring down at her, Lewis snarled, "Last chance." Her eyes glinted with mischief. No fucking way was he backing down. Then again, it didn't look like she wanted him to, either. *Fuck.* It didn't matter how many times he'd already had her. Right now, he needed to take her all over again. Show her exactly what was what. He scraped the tip of his fang along her throat, settled between her legs, her thighs opening for him. With a single thrust of his hips, he sank into the moist warm folds between her thighs. His breath expelled in a slow, steady hiss. Fuck. The heat at that sweet center of hers was like a flame he couldn't resist touching, tasting, teasing.

"Oh, gods," Alicia groaned. Her legs wrapped around his waist, locking in tight. As he drove into her, she rocked her hips, meeting him thrust for thrust. Heat enveloped his full, throbbing shaft. Each time they came together, her body conforming to his, she strained against the tight hold he had on her wrists. It only seemed to intensify the erotic agony etched into her exquisite features. Her silky blonde hair splayed out across the white sheets, almost blending into it. A complete contrast to the flush in her cheeks and the glow of pleasure in her sapphire blues.

Fuck, she was beyond gorgeous. The most stunning creature he'd ever had the pleasure of laying his eyes on. He would never get enough of her. The fire between them heightened, becoming all-consuming. Releasing her wrists, he buried his face in the crook of her neck. His arms came around her back as he pounded into her faster and harder. Her sex clenched, spasming around his shaft, milking him dry. Each orgasm was more potent than the last.

Several minutes passed before either of their bodies stilled. Lewis swept a strand of blonde from her face. In this quiet moment between them, their gazes locked onto one another, he realized she hadn't just melted the ice around his heart, but she silenced the rage buried in the depths of his soul. *Mate* echoed around his head. He kissed her softly on the lips.

Her sinfully beautiful mouth curved into a broad smile, lighting up her entire face. "I guess you were right. There was another one in there,"

Alicia teased.

"Never doubt me again," he retorted. His cock was well spent. Though he'd happily repeat this if the need arose. Or the desire overtook him. He didn't think he'd ever truly get enough of her. Rolling off of her, Lewis drew her to his side. Eventually, they'd need to get up, find some food, and figure out their next step.

"I won't make any promises." Her fingertips skimmed his abs, tracing the lines of his six-pack as if they were a piece of parchment. His stomach rumbled. Alicia allayed her hand. "Not the reaction I was expecting."

Given all the exercise they had and his injury, the timing seemed accurate. Their last meal occurred prior to their departure this morning. He expected hunger would come for her soon as well. "Did you check the pantry when you searched the cabin earlier?" With the sun now below the horizon, hunting was out of the question. Especially around these parts.

"No. It didn't cross my mind. Do you think it'll have something?"

"Possibly. Unless you can conjure up a meal, that's our only option."

"Magic doesn't work like that. I can't just summon something out of thin air. There's an exchange that happens."

That made sense. He'd never watched the Red Queen or how she manipulated things. The less time he'd been around that female, the better things were for him. Except Alicia had drawn the poison out of his body. What exchange occurred there? Lewis cast a glimpse in her direction. "Every time?"

"Mostly, yes. Sometimes it's as simple as a witch's own divine power. Other times, the exchange is bigger. Like with spells. They require a balance."

A balance? "Like a sacrifice." He felt her nod her head against his pecs. His eyebrows furrowed. That couldn't be accurate. The information he gathered on how to escape all pointed toward returning to the castle. Nothing about commuting something so they could leave. Shit. "So, a more potent spell, like an escape, demands something."

"Yes, but those usually have multiple stages, one building on another."

"Really?" Lewis scrubbed a hand across his face. Fuck. He'd overlooked something. Which meant defeating the worebeore was just their first step. Great. As if dealing with that creature wasn't hard enough. It now predicated their escape.

Her eyebrows shot up. "What the fuck is a worebeore?"

Shit. Had he said that out loud? Judging by the look of confusion written on her face, he had. No way he could walk it back now. "Do you remember that massive creature chasing you in the forest?"

Alicia blinked rapidly as if she had a difficult time processing his question. She visibly swallowed, cleared her throat, and snuggled closer to him, slipping the duvet over their bodies. "You mean the bear thing with spiked fur?"

"Yeah. That's a worebeore." Rubbing his thumb across his forehead, Lewis let out a heavy sigh. Although he referenced the thing unintentionally, the words were out there now. He might as well uncork the screw and let it all fly. The truth would've come out at some point. "You know I've been stuck here for a while. I've tried for years to find a way out. That's why I knew about Heart Tower. The books there never offered much, except that my only means was to defeat the worebeore. Then battling the witch."

Her head jerked up, her eyes snapping at him. "Witch? What witch?"

"The Red Queen." Right. He hadn't shared that tidbit of information either. Gods, this conversation would have started so much easier if he at least trusted Holloway's assessment. Then he would've given Alicia the benefit of the doubt. Nothing he could change now.

Alicia bolted upright, dragging the duvet with her and clutching it against her breasts. Her mouth slackened as she paled, struggling to find the words. She shook her head. "I'm sorry. I think I misunderstood. Are you telling me the Red Queen, the woman who… tormented you… is a witch?"

The pained stare etched on her lovely features tore him in half. It wasn't just the anguish burning in those bright blues, but the disbelief and… fear. Like he'd purposely hidden something noteworthy from her. In a sense, that's exactly what he'd done. All that time under the Red Queen's hold damaged him. That female had gone out of her way to break him.

And nearly succeeded. How could he explain that to Alicia?

"If I unchain you, will you run?"

Keeping his eyes on the dirt-covered floor, he shook his head. "No, mistress," Lewis declared, his voice rough and dry from lack of water. He had to bide his time; convince her he spoke only the truth. Otherwise, death would come for him before he ever got the chance to escape. And freedom would forever be out of reach.

"I don't believe you." Seizing his face, she forced his eyes upon her. Her sharpened nails dug into his cheeks. Blood trickled down his jaw. "You'll run the second you have the chance. Since your current punishments aren't enough, perhaps something worse will teach you a lesson." Her gaze shot over her shoulder as she shoved him back. "Bring the table in and chain him down."

Beating the unbidden memory back, Lewis sat up and dragged a hand through his dark hair. He peered out the window, catching small patches of the moonlight as it danced with the leaves. Gods, sometimes he'd give anything to be someone different. He blew out a shallow breath. There was no easy way to say it. "Yes." He swallowed to wet his parched throat. "The… the, uh… the Red Queen is a witch."

Clasping the soft fabric of the duvet to her bosom, she pushed up to her knees and stared at him. "And you didn't think to tell me? Don't you think something *that* important I should know?" Her voice cracked as she spoke.

Gods, she sounded so small. Nothing he said would make the situation better. Hell, he was liable to just make it worse. But he had to say something before she made assumptions. Lewis opened his mouth. Closed it. Opened. Shut it. He hung his head. No matter how he tried, words refused to come to him.

"You don't trust me," Alicia whispered.

Catching a whiff of the salty scent of tears, he lifted his head. Shit. He didn't intend to make her cry. As Lewis reached out, she shot out of the bed, muttering 'no' under her breath, shaking her head. "Alicia."

Without a word, she turned away from him. The white-knuckled grip she had on the thick blanket tightened as her shoulders hunched. Lewis climbed off the mattress and closed the distance between them. "That female is a part of my past. It's not something I talk about. It didn't cross my mind to share the things you should know." Hesitantly, he placed a tender hand on her shoulder, encouraging her to focus on him.

Brushing the tears from her cheeks, she lifted her chin high and hardened her gaze. "I can't fight an enemy if I don't know what I'm up against. And what if she's stronger than I am? What if I'm not powerful enough to defeat her and get us out of here?" Panic flared in her eyes. It was as if the words sunk in and took a strangled hold of her, steamrolling over whatever confidence she had found. Alicia paced back and forth in front of the couch as words tumbled out of her. "I'm not that remarkable. Everything fizzles out. The bonding ceremony would've changed that, but that'll never happen now. Because I left my engagement—"

A low, guttural snarl cut her off. A threaded pulse of energy exploded out of him. His hands cranked into tight fists. The idea of another male running their hands over her body, kissing her lips, tasting her tongue made him murderous. Tension fused into every limb as a fury he'd never known practically consumed him. Lewis grabbed the back of her neck and pressed a hard kiss to her lips, staking his claim. "Let's get one thing straight," he growled. "You're mine."

Drawing herself to her full height, she folded her arms across her chest and thrust her chin in the air. "One, I don't belong to anyone except myself. Two, my father arranged the engagement. It isn't something I wanted. Three, I choose who I want. So, lose the macho Tarzan attitude. Or our escape will be the least of your concerns."

Staring at her, he did a double take. Her reaction shouldn't have thrown him off, except no one ever spoke to him like that. Fuck if it didn't make him want to remind her who was boss. He cracked a grin. "You are mine. Deny it all you want, but it won't change the facts."

Her gaze narrowed at him. "That smile of yours won't woo me."

"It wasn't meant to, princess." At least not this time. They had other things to focus on right then. There would be plenty of time for the rest once they got out. "Now, I don't know about anything fizzling because you've held your own. Maybe give yourself a little more credit. Because I'm certain you're going to get us home."

Alicia opened her mouth and snapped it shut. Pivoting on the ball of her foot, she took a few steps and peered around the cabin, studying their surroundings. Nothing stood out. Crickets chirped in the background; a sharp breeze ruffled fallen leaves. It was the normal cadence of the forest. Halting her steps, she faced him, stroking her chin. "You might be right. Most spells don't require multiple witches. The more potent ones do, including something like an enchantment. We both got sucked into the egg. Perhaps I'm meant to be here. Because it's all about the spell. Which I'm thinking is linked to her."

"What do you mean?" If she got pulled into this on purpose, did that ring true for him as well? Fuck, he didn't even want to think about that.

"The Red Queen rules over the land, meaning this is her realm, but that doesn't mean she created it. I think it's her prison." Alicia half-shrugged. "I've only ever read about it, but when witches… go rogue… forget their role in the natural order, disrupting balance, you can't exactly strip a witch of her power. But you can imprison one. And there has to be a balance."

"So… two witches create that balance?" That sounded logical. Not that it explained how he fit into all of it.

"Yeah. And I think I know the spell that will get us home. Our path is just getting the items we need for it."

That left him with a lot of questions. Not so many answers. None of that mattered. He saw the first ray of light that he might actually get out of here. More than what he'd seen in the last twenty years. Lewis wrapped an arm around her waist and brushed a tender kiss across her nose and forehead. "Then let's see if we can't scrounge up some food and hit that spell book of yours. I don't know about you, but I'm ready to go home."

Alicia gave him hope.

Not just to break free from this world, but that he might have a future on the other side of that escape.

CHAPTER *Twelve*

"ARE YOU SURE about this?" Alicia raised an eyebrow as she cocked her hip to the side, dropping her hand to her waist. This idea of his wasn't a doozy, but it was definitely out there.

"Positive." Lewis yanked his tunic over his head, handing it over to her, and shucked each of his boots.

"Then why'd you bother getting dressed if you were just going to strip?" It sounded like a good question as it rolled out of her mouth. Truthfully, she knew why before he even answered. Their bodies had joined more times last night than she'd ever done in her life. And dear Lilith, it was fucking head-spinning. It had to be what women swooned about. Not that she ever spoke of sex with her friends. Shit. Not even her sister. And she didn't quite recall seeing the remnant of any kind of genuine satisfaction on her sister's part.

"Because if I hadn't, I would've had you under me in a heartbeat. Then where would be?"

"Naked and sweaty." With a slight smirk, she partially covered her mouth with her fingers. The words came out of their own volition. Though she certainly wouldn't take them back. She enjoyed seeing him come undone too much. A problem she never thought she would ever have.

His arm came around her waist, crushing her body to his as he claimed her lips in a hot, tongue-thrusting kiss. "Now be a good girl, princess. We won't exactly be able to communicate when I'm in my other form."

"Small favors."

"You're lucky there isn't time for me to punish you now, but I'll remember it later."

Heat flooded the apex of her thighs. Her core bloomed in anticipation. Seriously? Though the groan that came out of Lewis made it so worth it. "You have no one but yourself to blame for that," Alicia snickered. "You know how much I hate that moniker, yet you insist on using it."

"And that's why I use it."

Giving him a slight nudge, she stepped out of his arms. "Come on. Strip." While she wouldn't mind watching the last of the show, focusing on something else would get them further along. Alicia undid the latch on the leather satchel and added his tunic and boots to the small pile. She shrank his weapons before they even exited the cabin. They would've only impeded his other form. His trousers came into her line of sight. It took every ounce of control she could muster *not* to ogle his muscular form as she tucked them away with everything else.

A sharp crack jerked her head up. Lewis was on all fours. Two of his limbs popped out at unnatural angles. Without even thinking, she reached out as she took a step forward.

When it happens, don't approach. It will look… painful, but nothing you do will help. Or stop it.

Out of nowhere, his words replayed in her mind, stopping her feet.

Except in the heat of battle, we don't shift in front of… outsiders.

Despite the connection between them, she was still an outsider in his world. Just as he was one in hers. To her knowledge, supernaturals like them didn't interact. Which appeared wrong somehow. Vampires, shifters, witches… they all had one true common enemy—hunters. Not each other.

More bones snapped, yanking her out of her thoughts. His joints and limbs contorted, stitching into a new form. White fur with a few streaks of brown sprouted all over his body. Transfixed by the transformation, she watched with complete awe as his ears lengthened and he grew in height. She barely stood taller than him on all fours. His transition from his human form to his animal form seemed to draw on, though it likely only took a matter of seconds. Slowly, Alicia moved to stand in front of him. The same golden-brown eyes she'd stared into over the last several hours looked back at her. "Gods, you're stunning."

Lewis chuffed as if he agreed with her assessment.

Not only was he the first shifter she'd ever met, but he was the first she saw like this. It was completely humbling. Despite the appearance of a cute and fluffy jackrabbit, his claws and fangs suggested he could be deadly. Hesitantly, Alicia lifted a hand, reaching out. "May I?" The urge to touch him was strange. Then again, she was about to ride on his back.

Lowering his head, he pressed the top of his snout against her palm. The best kind of permission possible. Gods, his fur was long and soft, like silk tickling her skin. Though his pelt covered most of his body, his ears were hairless. Was that normal for his species? Maybe. Not that she imagined there were many jackrabbit shifters. Which meant, like her, he was different. He bumped his head gently against her hand, glanced over his shoulder, and lowered his belly to the ground.

"Right." They needed to get moving. Time was of the essence and they had a lot to accomplish. Ensuring she had her satchel locked, she hung it across her body. Hopefully, this would keep it out of the way. With a dip of her chin, she stepped around him, carefully climbed atop his back, and repositioned herself a few times. Once she settled and locked in, he shot off into the forest, darting around trees with immense power and speed.

As Lewis raced toward their destination, the greenery passing by them, her mind churned over the spell they discussed last night.

Delicately turning another page in the grimoire, Alicia took a bite of the salted pork and popped a square of cheese into her mouth. A few keywords stood out on the yellowed paper. "It's not this one, but we're close."

"How can you tell?"

"The ink is a bit more faded. These are among the oldest spells my faction has ever used." She just hoped it wasn't one of the restricted spells. Given how things went in her life—she flipped the page and sighed heavily.

"It's blank."

"No, it isn't." They simply couldn't see it yet. Eyeing the scattered mess covering the coffee table, she located his dagger and picked it up.

His eyes widened. "What are you doing?"

"Retrieving the spell." Without looking at him, Alicia pressed the tip of the blade into the center of her left palm until blood bloomed across her flesh. Her hand hovered over the weathered parchment as she squeezed it into a tight fist. Crimson dots fell, splattering onto the page, bringing it to life. From the center, words spilled forth like a faucet that wouldn't stop running. "Good news. I found the spell."

"Bad news?"

His question didn't surprise her. Because with a statement like that, how could bad news not follow? "It's worse than I thought."

What she found in those pages hadn't inspired—something colossal slammed into them, sending her flying from Lewis' back. She hit a nearby tree, knocking her breath out of her as she landed on the ground. Even as pain radiated up her calf, she glanced at Lewis, checking on him. His claws scraped against the earth as he skidded to a halt and shook off the hit.

Fuck. It was like a fucking monster truck plowed right into them. Rubbing the back of her head, Alicia chanced a look at what ran into them. A bear-like creature roared. Guess that answered that. He pawed at the grass and glowered at Lewis, who snarled in response. Hopefully, he realized she was okay. Mostly. As she tried to get to her feet, her right lower leg throbbed. "Fuck," Alicia grunted, her breath catching in the back of her throat.

Right. No standing. It didn't make her useless, but she couldn't be right in the center of the fight with the worebeore. Looked like Lewis got his wish after all. Just not in the way they previously agreed. Ignoring the pounding ache at the base of her skull, she focused on the conflict between Lewis and the worebeore. The two lunged at one another as a small group of soldiers came running around a massive tree trunk.

"Shit." At least she didn't have to sit on the sidelines. So to speak. Slapping her hands together, she rubbed her palms against one another, generating a large bout of energy as she mumbled a spell under her breath. Three of the guards raced toward her, notching arrows in their crossbows at her chest. Uttering the last resonance, she threw her hands out, turning the crossbows on the men at the moment the arrows released. The head of each arrow struck its owner, piercing them in the chin, shooting right through their cranium. Blood splattered everywhere as the bodies flopped to the ground.

While she couldn't repeat that particular spell, she had other tricks up her sleeve. No matter how many guards came at her, she would fight until the bitter end. Whatever it took to give Lewis his best chance at defeating the worebeore. As another set of soldiers approached, she summoned blood morning stars. Each left her fingers arching through the air, slicing through their intended targets. Three more bodies crumpled at her feet.

Then another set, staining the grass with more red. The battle between Lewis and the worebeore wore on. Both exhaling ragged breaths in their own right. Although it appeared the worebeore's strength waned, they couldn't keep this up forever. This went against everything they intended. Yes, in war, plans often changed on the fly, but she wanted them both to survive.

If she didn't do something, the soldiers would turn their focus from her to him. No way he could fight on both ends. That left her with one option. Alicia and Lewis locked eyes for a moment. In that second, they came to a silent accord, sealing their fate.

Alicia dug her nails into the dirt. Latching onto the earth, she combined that power with that of her own, the blood from her laceration seeping into the ground. Steaming ahead, words poured out of her mouth in a steady rhythm like the resolute flow of a river. A dark shroud encircled them, covering their actions from weak minds. Whatever soldiers came upon them now would see nothing. Not the small pile of dead mere yards from her or the battle between Lewis and the opposition.

Though she tried to track the fight, the spell required all of her attention. A glimpse here and there of claws, fangs, and thrashing gave her a decent picture. As an ache set up shop in her arms, Lewis flopped down in a patch of grass beside her. Gashes, bruises, and dried blood covered his naked human form. "Are you alright?" he asked between uneven puffs of air.

"I'm upright, but I don't know if I can hold this shroud any longer." Her lungs burned from the continuous stream of speech. The brief reprieve helped a little. Not that it lasted. Regarding the mangled worebeore lying motionless on the ground a few yards from them, she returned to the rote, locking down the concealment.

"I think we're okay." As if he comprehended the unspoken question on her lips, he tilted his head and closed his eyes, listening for the soldiers. Sitting up, his eyes popped open. "We're good. You can relax."

While she believed him, it was still risky. Neither of them could fight further. They needed time to heal and recover. But she couldn't hold the shroud any longer. Releasing the spell, her body slumped. Lewis caught her before she fell over. "I've got you. Don't worry. We won't stay here."

"Where… where will we go?" Where could they hide? He'd never gotten past this point before. They had speculated on options last night but came up with nothing conclusive.

"Well…" He blew out a heavy breath. "Can you stand?"

"No. I think my leg is broken." It wasn't the time or place for her to use a healing spell. Not that she had the energy right that second, either.

"Shit. Leaves us with one choice. One I prefer we avoided, but it's all we've got." Lewis propped her up against the tree and dug his trousers and boots out of her satchel.

Yeah. She knew exactly what he meant. *It's a tea party full of madness. They speak complete nonsense and seem forever stuck in the same moment.* 'Everyone has a little madness inside of them,' she told him. He hadn't appreciated that last night and she didn't think he'd care for her commentary now. Funny. When he mentioned the tea party, she got the sense they would find their way there. It seemed right up their alley. "At least we're not far from it."

"That isn't what worries me." His brows drew together as he yanked on his pants, did the buttons up, and then stuffed his feet into his boots.

No, it wasn't, was it? Nor that the soldiers would find them because that had happened multiple times. Did he think the tea party would turn them in? No. That wasn't it, either. She frowned as his hands fell to his waist and his gaze dropped to the ground. "You think we'll get sucked into whatever… loop they have going on, don't you?"

"Yeah. And we've come too far to get lost now. We're so close… I can almost taste it."

"Hey." Reaching up, she captured his hand in hers. They'd come so far. She refused to let anything stop them or get in their way. Hadn't they proven that already? "Nothing like that is going to happen."

His lips pressed into a thin line. "What makes you certain of that?"

She couldn't say how she knew, just that she did. But that wouldn't be enough. Just like she'd questioned his trust in her yesterday, he'd do the same. Though they'd proven to one another how much they trusted the other. Consistently. That was it, wasn't it? The answer. The corner of her mouth lifted in a faint smile. "Because we're together."

An answer that was both simple and complex. Just like them.

Lewis gritted his teeth as he took another step forward. He'd carried Alicia over the last couple of miles as they headed toward the one place he prayed they'd find help. Though she hardly weighed a thing, his injuries began surpassing his determination. Another spasm shot across his thigh. He stumbled around a large oak tree, weaving like a damn drunk.

"You need to put me down."

"Not yet. We're not close enough." Of course, that didn't matter. He intended to carry his precious load the entire way. She didn't need to put any weight on that leg. Regardless of what Alicia said, he could handle the pain racking his body. The agony lancing through him was just the adrenaline shot he required to move forward. They were old friends.

The aromatic scent of cinnamon and mulled cider tickled his nostrils. Voices nearby murmured. Not that any of it made a lick of sense. Laughter and spoons clicking against the side of a mug sounded over the din. Blowing out a soft breath, Lewis hobbled over to the nearest trunk and leaned against it. "We're close."

"Yeah. I can tell." Alicia grunted as he eased her out of his arms and repositioned her so she used him as a crutch. "What the hell is an un-birthday?"

"I've got no clue. You'll have to ask them. Provided you can get a straight answer." Which he suspected she wouldn't. Once he had her situated, they hobbled along together, taking their time to approach. His eyes zeroed in on the long table surrounded by wrought-iron chairs. Only a few people filled the padded seats. Pots of sugar, milk, and other spices lay scattered across the shiny surface. A selection of colorful fruit tarts, cakes, and pies sat piled high atop a serving dish. A plate of toast and jam sat in front of each of those gathered. Not that he recognized any of them. Though he heard rumors regarding each, they'd never met.

A pale-faced male at the head of the table jumped on top of it. He ambled across the table, not minding in the least he jumbled jars of jam and knocked over sugar containers as he strode toward them. Hopping down to the ground, he landed with a slight thud in front of them, his gaze locking on Alicia. "It's Alice," he called over his shoulder. "I'd know them anywhere."

"That's not *our* Alice."

"It's the wrong one."

"Yes, it is. I have fitted that head many times." The male stretched out his hands, hovering them over the crown of Alicia's head as if he were measuring it. "Oh, yes, it is—"

A low growl rumbled in his chest. Baring his teeth, he snapped at the male. The guy got too close to her for his liking. This piece of shit needed to back off before he lost a limb. Alicia rested a comforting palm against his pec. The skin-on-skin contact eased him. It was insane, the control she had over him with nothing more than a touch.

With a quiet yelp, the male jerked his hands back. "Perfect match." He glanced at the two seated around the table. "It's their un-birthday. They always visit on their un-birthday."

"What's an un-birthday?" Alicia asked.

"See. Not our Alice. She doesn't even know what an un-birthday is."

"Not our Alice," the other nodded fanatically. It's head bobbing up and down like a bobble-head toy.

"But we must always remind them of their un-birthday. They are quite forgetful."

"I am not," Alicia retorted defiantly. "My name is Alicia. Not Alice."

The other two creatures jumped up and down screaming, 'Not Alice,' in a sing-song manner. Lewis inhaled and exhaled a deep breath. How fucking long did he allow this to continue? This didn't accomplish a damn thing. His impatience grew thinner by the minute.

"That is a very Alice thing to say." The male grinned widely. A serious look crossed his pale features. "Why is a writing desk like a raven?"

Dear gods, these creatures irritated him. He didn't miss a damn thing by avoiding this lot. Rubbing his thumb and forefinger across his forehead, he pinched the bridge of his nose. Maybe it would help stave off the oncoming headache. "We need some help."

"That you do," Holloway stated, his purple and blue body rotating as he appeared out of nowhere. "The cards are coming."

"Fucking hell." He never should've agreed to this. They couldn't turn back now. Blatantly ignoring the two idiots running around like their pants were on fire, Lewis eyed Alicia, noting the way her shoulders slumped. She carried a lot of weight for them throughout this adventure. "You can't use your magic right now, can you? Make us invisible? Shrink us?"

"Invisibility requires a concentrated connection between the two of us. While I think we can pull it off, I'm not sure I'd want to risk it with both of us injured. And shrinking… I've only ever done that on objects. Not… people."

"It's okay." Lewis brushed a tender kiss across her forehead. "We'll find another way." He could tell her inability to protect them bothered her. Not that he'd have it. She didn't deserve that.

"The tea," the pale-faced male declared. "It is tea time. A perfect time to have tea and crumpets. And then we shall act un-normal."

"You're right," Holloway tacked on before Alicia or Lewis could object. "Have some tea, then the Hatter can place you in the pot until the cards are gone."

Hatter? Who the fuck was the Hatter? Unless… Lewis cocked an eyebrow. He narrowed his gaze on the pale-faced male dressed in a blue-and-green jacket, wool pants, a patterned vest, fingerless cotton gloves, an oversized hat, and a silk bowtie. Yeah. That made sense. That meant the other two were the hare and the dormouse. None of the information he gathered distinguished one from the other. As maddening as those three were, Holloway hadn't steered him wrong yet. "Fucking hell. Let's have some tea."

While the hatter and his two companions worked on two steaming mugs of tea, Lewis got Alicia settled into a chair. They both needed off their feet, but he didn't want her to shrink and fall over, damaging that leg more. Gods, he loathed every part of this. Working with the morons anyway. Being around Alicia, spending time with her, having her on his back… he liked all of that. Not something he'd ever expected. Her presence alone did things to him he never imagined possible.

They each sipped from the cups presented to them. Shrinking to an unnatural size felt similar to the hum he'd sensed when Alicia made them invisible. It was like a static threading across his skin. Within seconds of them reaching their reduced size, the Hatter collected them and placed them together inside a tea pot.

"This isn't what I expected," Alicia commented.

"Me either." At least they were protected. Sitting down against the cool porcelain, he tucked her into his side, wrapping her in his arms. Lewis pressed his nose to the top of her head, drinking in her naturally luxurious scent. Yeah, he would never get enough.

"Still think they're mad?"

"They might be safe, but they're absolutely mental." Random shouting matches, screaming for no reason, running around like lunatics. It all fit the bill.

"Maybe." She pressed her lips to the underside of his jaw. "But I'll tell you a secret."

Lewis lifted his head and cocked an eyebrow at her. A secret? Oh, he couldn't wait to hear this. "What's that?"

"The best people are."

She might just be right about that. Some might call them mental. And he was perfectly alright with that. The sound of loud, demanding voices echoed outside of the tea pot. With the thickness of the container blocking them, he only caught a few muffled words here and there. One thing was for certain. The guards had caught up with them. As had the knave.

Closing his eyes, Lewis shut out all the other noises and focused solely on the voices.

"You haven't seen a blonde-haired female and the rabbit?"

"There is a difference between a rabbit and a hare. While the latter drinks tea, I don't know of the former. Though it seems rather ridiculous to compare the two. They are so alike. And all friends are welcome. It is a tea party. Would you care for some tea?"

"No! I'd like you to answer the damn question!" The teapot jumped as something slammed down against the table. Lewis tightened his hold on Alicia as it quickly stilled. *Shit.* That was closer than he liked.

"The response in and of itself is an answer."

"There's nothing here, sire."

"Consider yourselves lucky."

Several minutes of silence passed before someone lifted the lid from the teapot. The hatter poked his head over them. "The unkindly man has departed with the cards."

"Take them to your home, Hatter," Holloway stated. "Give them food and rest. Tomorrow is a big day for them."

"Yes, of course," Hatter replied. "Anything for Alice."

Lewis couldn't agree more. Anything for Alicia.

CHAPTER *Thirteen*

"WHAT DO YOU mean you couldn't tell if they were there?"

Jaq glowered at Carter as if she'd grown a second fucking head. How the hell else did his statement not register? Or had all the millennia destroyed that once impressive gray matter of hers? Either way, he couldn't make things any clearer. "I said what I said." Too many scents had mingled together and started smelling the same after a while. At that damn tea party, he couldn't differentiate one from the other. The only one he knew for sure was the rabbit's stench. He hadn't caught a whiff of it anywhere around that place. And they'd lost track of the trail of blood. It cut off somewhere in the forest, offering them no sense of direction traveled.

"So, we have no clue where they've gone?"

"No, but we are well aware of where they've been. That includes defeating the worebeore." His men located the creature's carcass about ten feet from a pile of dead soldiers. They tossed all of them in a pyre, burning them where they took their final breaths. Such a waste.

"That helps how exactly?" Carter snapped. "Without knowing where they are, I don't know how much farther they have to go. So fucking what they killed that damn creature? They could make their way here in a roundabout way, throwing everything I have planned for tomorrow night off track."

Jaq folded his arms across his chest. Of course, she made this shit about her. Like he should've expected differently after all these years together. "Then cancel the fucking party."

"Not happening." Disgust twisted her pretty mouth into a sneer. "Make your men useful and find me my prize."

Clenching his jaw, he narrowed his gaze, his body going rigid. Who the fuck did she think she was ordering him around like this? Yeah, called herself a queen, but it didn't fucking make her one. Not in this realm. Or any other. "No." Jaq got in close, invading her personal space, and smirked.

"Excuse me?" Her eyes widened, the whites showing. She jabbed a finger in his face. "That wasn't a request. Now do as you're told."

"No." Gods, that word felt fan-fucking-tastic. Who knew a word could give him such a thrill? And one as simple as that. It held far more power than he dared to dream about.

A quick, sharp blow landed across his cheek as her palm connected with his face. His head jerked with the slap. The sting barely registered. Carter shook with fury. "I'm in charge. My rules control your livelihood. You'll do as you're ordered."

His hand shot out, wrapping around that slim neck of hers. Slamming her against the stone wall, he tightened his grip and pressed his face close to hers. "You're nothing but a powerless witch." The last time they'd done this, he'd fucked her hard. Now the very thought made his stomach turn. "I remember what got us in this predicament. Everything that I lost because of you. Not a mistake I'll make again."

Her feet dangled, kicking against the wall, as she smacked at his arm. "You... need... me."

Words he heard before. It was what looped him into this whole damn show in the beginning. Did he really *need* her now? She'd already executed the spell, linking it to that heart on the altar. Once the witch stabbed it with the athame, he was fucking free. What the hell did he need this bitch for? *Not a damn thing.* "Says who?" A wicked grin crossed his face as he squeezed her throat tighter. He could kill her right now. Save them all some fucking trouble.

Those dangling feet of hers scrambled harder against the stone as she fought against his hold, smacking and slapping at him. "En…chant…ment…link…to…me…"

"No!" he snapped. That couldn't be right. It just couldn't. Loosening his grip ever so slightly, he replayed what he recalled of that night.

"What were you thinking?" his brother, his alpha, asked.

"They're just humans. Filthy sheep. That's what you called them, Nasim," he retorted. Why did it matter if he killed them? It was nothing more than an exchange of goods. A barter between him and the witch.

"And it led to the deaths of three witches." Nasim slashed his hand in the air, cutting off his rebuttal. "Even if that hadn't occurred, we're still sworn to protect humans. They aren't fodder for our war. Do you truly not comprehend the damage you've caused?"

His eyebrows drew together. No. That couldn't be right. Carter… she would've told him if those deaths went beyond anything more than a grab for power. They both wanted to overthrow those in charge. A desire that had landed him here. He glanced at the chains that bound his wrists. A rumble percolated in his chest as he glowered at his brother from under low lids. "You lie," he declared. It wouldn't be the first lie the male had told, all of them at his expense.

Nasim shot to his feet, yet hesitated in any other action as he clenched his fists. "That witch has done a number on you, brother. Are you so loyal it has made you blind? She doesn't care about you. You're nothing but a pawn to her."

"Rule has been made on the witch. She's being imprisoned in an enchantment, locking her life to it," the beta said as he approached from behind. "Helena asks if you have decided what to do with him?"

His brother dipped his chin, acknowledging the request. "Since you seem so inclined to this witch, perhaps you should share in her fate." Nasim glanced at the beta. "Tell Helena to do what she will. And deliver the same punishment to him. Take him away."

Motherfucker! If he killed her now, his chance of escape would disappear. That was the last thing he wanted. He'd wait. Once they were free, her life was fair game. Jaq released his hold, letting Carter crumple to the ground. "This is only a reprieve," he growled as she rubbed her throat, coughing, struggling to catch her breath. He crouched down on his haunches and squared his shoulders as a fevered stare settled on his features. "I loathe you. So, deal with the cards yourself. Get them to do your bidding, because I won't play your puppet any longer." Rising to his full height, he pivoted on the ball of his foot and stalked off, leaving the bitch to her own devices.

Alicia stifled a giggle as Lewis scrunched his nose. "You're not supposed to smell it." The hatter got them safely to his small, slightly cramped home, returned them to their correct height, and took off. It surprised her that he left them alone in his home, but to each their own.

"So, it should reek?"

"At the start, yes. It'll shift once it's brewing." She cracked a soft smile as Lewis added the herbs, spices, and other dry ingredients into the iron pot hanging over the hearth. Water began bubbling. Soon, they'd have a healing potion to address their injuries. Although the slashes, bites, and bruises covering his body had re-knitted themselves, his left leg still wasn't right. Nor was hers, for that matter. Lewis helped her reset the bone, but that only partially resolved the issue.

While he mixed everything together, she surveyed the house. It was similar to one of those miniature homes people talked about. Same size, just a lot of hats, materials, books, gadgets, and devices she didn't recognize. With two stories. The rickety staircase led to a loft-style bedroom with one king-sized bed. The hatter told them they were welcome to it. According to him, he didn't use it. Instead, the male slept on the long couch, staying close to his hats and tools.

"How will I know this is done?"

"Stir it ten times counterclockwise. Once it turns turquoise, it's finished." Alicia stared at Lewis, silently counting as he stirred. He pulled his tunic on after their arrival. Not so much to hide his wounds or the tattoos, but as a protection. Possibly from her magic? Or the components of the spell? She wasn't sure. Except Lewis had put it all together since she couldn't stand. He had retrieved the pestle and mortar, along with all the other elements they had required from the kitchen, to make the healing potion. No argument. No fight. Did he realize even his shifter abilities would go so far? Or was it all for her?

His eyebrows furrowed as he stole a sidelong glance at her. "Am I doing it wrong?"

"No. You're fine." Her mind churned as the potion brewed, its color changing from sunburst orange to a lilac purple. As the liquid magic continued its transformation, she eyed Lewis. Despite all the injuries the worebeore gave him, not once had she seen a hint of pain cross his features. It was the same when he shifted. Did he even feel it? "Can I ask you something?"

"I won't stop you."

"What's it like when you shift? Does it hurt?"

Lewis paused for a second. His gaze flicked from her to the pot as he resumed stirring. "No matter which form I take, every bone in my body breaks and stitches back together. The first shift… is pure agony. It's like someone continuously taking a hot iron to every part of your body. But the more you do it, the easier it gets until one day when you no longer notice the pain. At that point, it's just second nature. You're a witch. I'm sure you go through something, too."

"Yeah. Sort of." Though nothing like what he described. Still, he shared with her. She wanted to do the same. "Learning spells is the easy part. Our innate power is like a second puberty. We generally experience both simultaneously. As our bodies are changing, so, too, are our powers. While we can learn other skills during that time, the focus is always on our innate magic. It takes years to truly master."

"Until your reaction becomes automatic, right?"

"Right." Alicia glimpsed at the potion. "That's finished." The liquid turned a beautiful, sparkling turquoise. "Let me find a couple of vials." She pressed her palms against the arms of the chair she occupied.

"I'll find them." Setting the wooden spoon aside, he gestured to the chair. "You stay seated."

"I can help." An injury didn't make her an invalid. Was it necessary for her to sit here and do nothing? Especially since they should bottle a few vials up. It made sense to keep it handy. The war wasn't over for them.

"Absolutely not." His eyebrows pinched together as his mouth contorted into a scowl. "You'll sit there like a good girl while I take care of things. Got it?"

A flush of heat speared through her. That look on his face wasn't sexy. *Oh, yes, it fucking is.* Grinding her teeth, she crossed her arms. "I hate being told what to do."

"Liar," he growled. Desire glinted in those liquid gold orbs, intensifying the blaze gripping her core.

Fuck. Sex should be the last thing on her mind. They had other things to address, like locating the athame, and determining the best route into the castle. Yet all she could think about was getting him naked. Maybe it had to do with the way he spoke to her. Or that they had survived their first battle. Or that their escape was actually within reach. Either way, she yearned to get her hands on him.

Alicia watched as Lewis prowled around the kitchen, scouring the cabinets for a couple of small glass containers. His limp was hardly noticeable as he moved about. Stopping in front of a floor-to-ceiling cupboard, his eyes narrowed. He plucked two circular tubes from inside and held them out toward her. "Will these do?"

"Yeah. Just don't get it on your hands as you spoon it into them." They were too small for him to dunk them into the mixture, meant for ingestion only. She fixated on his every step, monitoring him in case anything went wrong. Bum leg or not, she wouldn't let any kind of magic cause him harm.

Lewis took tremendous caution as he scooped the potion into the tiny vials and then he carefully carried them over to where she sat, presenting her with one and joining her on the couch. "Bottoms up?"

"Pretty much." They each knocked their container back, taking the potion like a shot of liquor. It burned a touch as it went down her throat, roiling in her stomach, warming her from the inside out. The swill circulated through her system, stretching and clawing its way across every nerve-ending in her body, repairing the broken bone and lighting her up as bright as the moon.

Holy shit. Without conscious thought, Alicia launched across the sofa, throwing her arms around Lewis' neck, fusing their lips together. He plied the seam of her mouth open with the velvet warmth of his tongue. With a fiery determination, he scooped her up, squeezing her ass hard as he stood. She groaned into the kiss, her legs naturally coming around his waist. Fuck, he tasted like pure, raw magic.

That magnificent bulge of his pressed into her lower belly. While she expected they'd have another repeat of last night, she hadn't thought it would happen like this. His large thighs ate the distance as he climbed the staircase, each step creaking underneath his feet. Not that he slowed down in the slightest. Nor did she want him to.

Lewis carried her across the room without breaking the kiss and laid her down on the mattress. The cool covers brushed against her shoulders as their mouths separated. "Strip," he growled as he gripped her upper leg. "Because I'll rip your only set of clothes to shreds if I do it."

Heat pooled at the apex of her thighs. Fuck, she enjoyed the hell out of that. "Something to remember for another time." When she had something else to wear. He stepped back and, with great urgency, he yanked his tunic over his head as she worked the ties of her corset with quick precision. It seemed neither of them could wait.

Each part of their outfits went flying, landing somewhere on the wooden floor. Lewis pressed a knee to the bedding, the mattress dipping as his naked form hovered over hers. His sweet, warm breath lingered just above her. Their lips locked together. He devoured her mouth with deep, sweeping strokes of his tongue.

Groaning into the kiss, passion overtook them. Their bodies came together like a car crash. Alicia dug her nails into his shoulders and hooked her legs over his hips. That was all the invitation he needed. Greedily deepening the kiss, Lewis angled the head of his cock at her entrance, gripped her thighs, and in a single thrust, filled her to the hilt.

Neither of them took a second. They didn't wait for her body to adjust to his girth. Lewis drew his hips back and pumped into her as she rose to meet him, stroke for stroke. Her body ignited in all kinds of delicious ways. It was like every receptor came alive, bursting with energy. The communion between their flesh sent a blaze straight to her core, lightning her nerve endings on fire. Her thighs tensed as his rhythm became frantic. In an explosion of stars, a hot jet shot into her, setting off her own waves of pleasure. Their mouths parted as they both cried out in pure ecstasy.

Lewis pounded into her as they rode out their mutual orgasms. Once it peaked, he only stilled for a moment before he curled one hand around her back and gripped her ass with the other. Somehow, he kept them conjoined as he rolled over onto his back. "Take me." As if his words required no other explanation, he reclaimed her lips in a passionate kiss that took her breath away. It was as if he had staked a claim on her.

Hooking her feet under his thighs, Alicia rocked back, sliding up and down his thick shaft. Whatever frenzied need surged through them left the room. With the way their bodies melded together now, something larger was at play. That perhaps, for the first time in each of their lives, they truly opened themselves up to… possibility.

As she continued a slow and steady rhythm, she skimmed her fingers up his forearms and across his biceps, learning the lines of every taut muscle. His hands roamed over her waist and back, exploring her dips and curves.

Tingles shot through her. His delicate touch lit her up in a way she'd never felt before. The gentleness was a complete contrast to his large body.

Although his hips rose to meet hers, Lewis let her set the pace. It was like he offered himself to her. As if this time between them was all about her. Pressing her palms to his pecs, Alicia dug her nails into his flesh as she sat up and increased her rhythm, swinging her hips faster, taking them both to that sweet, illustrious oblivion.

Despite the number of times they had come together yesterday and last night, everything about this exchange was different. It went beyond flesh-to-flesh. They reached one another on a deeper level. Mind-to-mind. Soul-to-soul. When their bodies blew apart, it was simultaneous. An all-consuming orgasm thundered through them. And gods, it was exquisite.

Alicia slowly stilled, settling her weight against him. Their gazes locked on one another. What she saw shining in those golden-brown orbs of his filled her heart with joy. She could see the future. And it was beautiful. With ragged breaths, she collapsed onto his chest. A sheen of sweat made it glow.

 Rolling off of him, she groaned as his cock slipped free from her and he tucked her into his side. That came out of nowhere. Possibly a side effect of the potion. Seemed like a rational explanation. Except it should speed up the recovery process, not throw them into an overload of lust. A spike of adrenaline, maybe? "I'm sorry. I don't know what came over me."

"Don't apologize. That was… incredible. You can do that *anytime* you want."

Her brows shot up as she sat up a bit. "I thought…" It was too much to hope she heard him wrong. They'd agreed to go their separate ways once they got free.

"What? Thought you'd get rid of me?" A broad smile crossed his face, revealing the tips of his canines. "Like I said, you're mine. And I'm never letting you go."

"Good." Alicia caressed his jaw and brushed a soft kiss across his lips. "I wouldn't have it any other way." As she straightened, her eyes landed on the lip of a panel protruding from the wall. Stopping short, she did a double-take. "What the hell?" Carefully, Alicia crawled over Lewis' chest, inspecting it more closely.

"What?"

"I don't know." Closing the distance, she scrutinized the line she noticed. It appeared out of place. An edge of some kind. But to what? Alicia ran her fingertip along the fringe. Hitting the corner, the panel cracked with a soft hiss. Her eyes widened as the glint of steel came into view. "Holy shit."

Lewis got to his knees and came up behind her. "What the hell is that?"

Reaching into the hidden case, her fingers curled around the ivory hilt. It had a set of sapphires, emeralds, and rubies embedded in it. Just as the picture in the grimoire showed. "It's the athame." They had the last piece.

They could kill the Red Queen.

And escape Wonder.

CHAPTER
fourteen

CARTER SCOWLED AS she regarded the endless guests spinning around
on the dance floor. Elaborate gowns and glittering jewelry adorning the
females sparkled beneath the hanging chandeliers. Fashioned to outdo
the next. Even the males competed with one another. The tails of their
tuxedos were long. Some had other décor lining either the coattails or the
lapels of their jackets. None of it garnered her attention. She drummed
her fingers against her chair's velvety arm.

Where the fuck was Jaq?

He should be right by her side, enjoying the fruition of their plan.
Everything had come together. Or so she believed. The fucking cards had
once again failed in their job and hadn't brought her the confirmation she
sought. Regardless of their argument last night, Jaq should have handled
that oversight.

His declaration against her couldn't be real. No fucking way he meant
that shit. Not after all of their time together. Yet she hadn't seen him since
that fight. Where the fuck was he?

Another couple approached and showed her the respect she deserved.
Just as many others had upon their arrival. Not something she'd miss.

Carter waved them off, sending them on their way. Rinse and repeat.

With a dismissive snort, she surveyed the celebration. Laughter and chatter rose above the chamber quartet, playing another instrumental. As if that would drown out the sheep droning on about their insignificant lives. Or the high heels clacking against the marble floor with each step those highbred debutantes took. Her pulse quickened as she pursed her lips. Lilith, she needed to get out of this room before she laid fire to these troglodytes.

Carter stood, descending the short staircase from her staged throne. Steeling her shoulders, she fingered the heart-shaped key dangling from the choker around her throat. The satin of her dress slid across her skin as she strolled across the room, seeking a server. A goblet of wine might ease her irritations. She eyed her handmaidens hovering nearby and barely bit back a hiss. If those whores were smart, they'd leave her be.

An attendant rushed over to her and presented a goblet of mulberry wine to her. "Your Majesty," he said, bowing low.

With a grunt, she accepted the proffered drink. The second she took it from his hand, he scurried off. Yeah. They all seemed to recognize she was in a foul mood. Carter sipped from the chalice; the tart notes were delectable on her tongue.

"Excuse me, Your Majesty," a member of her guard uttered on approach.

"What?" she snapped. Her temper had just begun settling. The few sips of wine doing its job. Only an idiot would chance an interaction with her right now.

"I hate to interrupt, but we have a situation."

Although given a chance to continue, the male said nothing further. "Spit. It. Out."

The guard leaned in close. "We have some unexpected visitors… down below."

"Oh? Care to elaborate?"

With the insurmountable number of guests floating about, some of them could've found their way to her dungeons. As the male offered a description of the intruders, a broad smile settled on her features. Didn't that just brighten her mood? "Let them in. Hold my guests here. Remove all cards from the throne room."

"Your Majesty?"

"Just do it." With that, Carter weaved through the crowd, bobbing around idiots who deemed it necessary to get in her way as she headed toward the exit. There was only one way out of the dungeons—a winding staircase that led to the throne room. What better place to fight another witch? Especially one of her own bloodline. Perhaps that worthless dragon would appear before their enemies arrived. He couldn't get out of here without her. Something she'd made perfectly clear.

And time was of the essence.

Lewis stalked forward. The foul stench of sewage and rotting flesh reached his nostrils. Gods, he forgot how bad it smelled in this place. Water dripping echoed off the stone walls as he eyed the corridor ahead. He glanced over his shoulder at Alicia. She was far too close to his liking, but they'd agreed on how to proceed. As much as he hated the idea of her fighting anyone, especially the Red Queen, they each had their own battle.

The thought of her getting involved in this at all made his skin crawl. Except she was a fearsome fighter. And there was no way he could deal with a dragon and the witch on his own and still get them out of Wonder in one piece. He just needed to stick to their plan. Dipping his muzzle, he gestured to the right-side narrow corridor. That would lead them to their first primary location—the prison cells.

He remained alert to anything beyond rattling chains and the labored breathing of prisoners. Nothing stood out. Not even as they approached the first cell. No guards. No attendants slipping food to the captives. No one receiving a punishment. What was wrong with this picture? It was far too easy to for them to have gotten as far as they did. And it wasn't as if he could call out, 'Here, dragon, dragon.' Like the male was a pet or some shit.

Stopping in front of the chamber, they peered through the iron bars. Light from the nearby torch flickered across a female's pale face. Lewis padded backward, giving Alicia room to work. With the flick of her wrist, the manacles and lock of the heavy wooden door clinked, swinging open. He studied the corridor, waiting for the creaking noise to draw attention, except nothing happened. No one came toward them.

At all.

He didn't like this. Not one fucking bit. A soft hand came upon his shoulder; long, delicate fingers sifting through his fur, calming him. Despite the ease of Alicia's touch, Lewis remained vigilant. Anything or anyone could've hidden between the cloak of night or the cover of the shadows all over the dungeon.

Not a damn thing changed as they repeated this process, releasing one bare-footed captive after another. One prisoner aided others in their escape, each muttering their thanks to him and Alicia upon their departure. Still, nothing out of the ordinary assaulted his senses. Out of his periphery, he eyed Alicia. Although she appeared just as dumbstruck, she constantly scanned their surroundings. They reached the servants' staircase without issue.

"Up there?" Alicia whispered.

Lewis nodded. Her hand cupped his jaw, a simple gesture telling him to be careful. He leaned into her lingering touch, reciprocating the unspoken exchange. With a dip of her chin, Alicia pivoted on the back of her heel and ascended the winding set of stone steps, disappearing from his sight.

His head jerked toward a faint whoosh. Fixating in the sound's direction, a steel blade sliced through the air. Lewis zeroed in on a hard, angular jaw and a pair of dark-brown eyes. The male hid himself well. Why wait? Or had Jaq approached while he watched Alicia head up the staircase?

Jaq took a step closer, swinging the sword in his hand in a slow circle. "I won't attack, if that's what you're waiting for."

His hackles rose. Yeah, like he trusted the male. The guy was no better than the queen and just as much of a liar. Stationing himself at the base of the staircase, Lewis growled a warning. A fight was inevitable, but the longer he stalled, the farther away Alicia got.

"I don't want to fight you, but I will if necessary. I'll even prove it." The male unlocked a nearby cell, releasing a prisoner, who took advantage of the situation and scampered off.

What the fuck? What kind of stunt was this? Was it a distraction of some kind? Similar to what he and Alicia planned. Set the prisoners free, drawing guards away from the throne room. No. No way he believed what happened. Lewis prowled forward, snarling at the male.

"She's your mate. I get it. You want to protect her." Raising a single hand as if in defeat, Jaq backed up. "At least I understand where you're coming from. Never had that myself. And no… Carter isn't my other half."

Lewis fixed the male with a hard stare, covering whatever confusion settled in his head with rage. This hadn't gone as he expected. The words coming out of Jaq's mouth made no damn sense.

"I used to think she was, but then I realized I never actually loved that bitch. That's not really important right now. What matters is that we're not going—you know, this would be so much easier if you shifted. Did you really expect us to go at each other? Beast to beast? We both know if that happened, I'd kill you. You'd be nothing more than a snack for me."

Not necessarily. Yeah, Jaq outmatched him in size. And strength. But he had speed. He could've outrun the male for a bit. Long enough to have accomplished his and Alicia's goal. That wasn't the point. It served him better if he stayed in his animal form.

"Come on, rabbit. Shift. I don't give a fuck that you'll be naked." Jaq grumbled under his breath. His words were undiscernible. "Killing you doesn't work for me. I've got other plans, which means I need you alive. But… perhaps we need to even things out." Swinging the sword in a wide arc, the male unsheathed a second blade from his back and sent it skittering across the dirt floor toward Lewis.

What was this guy's game? Maybe if he played along, he'd get some answers. Nothing the male uttered or did made a lick of sense. At least now he had a weapon. If need be, he could retake his animal form at a moment's notice. Lewis shifted to his human form, rising to his full height of six foot five, and curled his fingers around the blade's hilt at his feet. "Anyone ever tell you that you talk a fucking lot?"

"No, can't say they have, but as I said, I'm not interested in killing you."

"Care to elaborate?" If the male wanted to spit shit out, who the fuck was he to stop him? It might prove useful, even at this juncture. The two of them slowly circled one another.

"No. Not really. I will tell you that my plan changed. Not a lot for you to go on, but that's all I'm willing to share."

"Then it seems like we're at an impasse. Just because you have no desire to kill me doesn't mean we're on the same page. So, release all the prisoners you want or keep chattering on, but no matter what… I don't believe you." Maybe he couldn't defeat Jaq, as the male put it, beast to beast. But he could beat him in hand-to-hand or sword-to-sword, even without clothing or armor.

Jaq peered around the dungeon as if they had an audience. His mouth twisted into a sadistic grin. "Then we better make it look good."

Lewis swung the sword in a circle, adjusting his grip on the hilt, preparing to attack, and encircled Jaq. Did the male actually believe this was a performance? Then again, maybe to Jaq it was, but not to Lewis. Any fight, especially those during his time in Wonder, was all life or death. This was no different. Except this time, he had one hell of a reason to live. A witch with her golden locks splayed out across his bare chest flashed briefly in his mind.

Yeah.

One *hell* of a reason.

Alicia lingered in the archway, hidden by a massive suit of armor. A knight dutifully protecting the servants' corridor, exiting and entering the throne room. Sidestepping the pile of tin wasn't the wisest idea, but she couldn't see around it otherwise. Although she didn't have the key yet, she needed to discern where to go. A potent source of magical energy pulsated from the other side.

Using the suit to her advantage, she peeked into the small but resplendent throne room. When Lewis told her where the staircase led, this wasn't what she pictured. A stately throne of gold, covered in baroque crests, with ornate legs sat on the far side of the room. A red rug ran from the throne down the center and looped back from both left and right, allocating placement for those seeking an audience with the queen. Pointed banners with red hearts and golden edges adorned the walls.

To the right of the staging area, where the throne sat, was another archway framed by curtains, the same red as the banners. She sensed a source of magic behind it. That had to be where they'd find their escape hatch, so to speak.

"It's not polite to lurk," a feminine voice stated, bouncing off the walls.

Where the fuck had that come from? Scrutinizing the opulent columns, Alicia eyed the warm oranges and dancing shadows produced by the massive braziers that covered the hall. One of them concealed her enemy. "Who said I was lurking? Maybe I was just taking it all in." Adjusting her satchel, she sharpened her senses and sent out feelers to locate the Red Queen.

"By hiding behind a block of metal?" The female snorted. "Come now. You didn't think you'd trespassed on my land without my knowledge, did you?"

"Naturally." Guards had chased her all over Wonder, but the woman knew that. Then why mention it? Unless… "It's why you cast the spell a few days ago." Which meant the female did it—separated her heart from her body. And the tremendous source she felt behind those crimson curtains was the woman's heart. Alicia stepped out from behind the suit, noting the tiny flickers of magic intended to throw her off. Not that it worked. She zeroed in on the column, camouflaging the female.

"I've waited a long time for this. Oh, kin of my blood." The Red Queen sauntered out into the vast hall. A floor-length red ballgown with a massive train covered the female, trailing behind with each step taken.

The corset hugging the female's curves had diamond studs sewn into it, perfectly offset by the choker at the queen's throat. And the heart-shaped key dangling from it.

"Are you sure about that? Last I checked, I didn't have any cold-blooded snakes in my line." Though it explained how she sensed the power that thrummed in the woman. Along with everything else. Someone in her faction had created this world. That meant she could destroy it. Discreetly, Alicia summoned a ball of an electrical charge in her palm.

"So unladylike. I almost thought we were of similar mind. Now I see I was wrong." The heels of her shoes clicked against the marble floor as she strolled around the room, slowly closing the distance between them. "Tell me… what does the rabbit see in you? I don't imagine it's your mouth. Perhaps you're just a body to warm him." The queen traced a lone long finger down her collarbone. "We both know you'll never compare to me. After all, I *did* have him first."

A strange growl reverberated off the walls as Alicia lobbed the sphere of energy at the queen. Had Lewis made his way here? Or had something else joined in the fight? She didn't see a thing. Just the queen parrying the blast, which dispersed outward, fracturing pillars and splintering the walls. The vibration intensified. *Shit!* That sound came from her.

Not that she had more than a second to think about it. A clap of lightning barreled her way. Catching the force in her hand, she diverted it, simulating live butterflies which scattered into the non-existent wind. Simultaneously, Alicia shaped a charge and blood shurikens. One would strike from the front, while the other assaulted the queen from the side.

Alicia shot a flurry of electric arrows. Though the queen dodged most of them, one was a direct hit, center mass. The female staggered a few steps just as the pointed end of a shuriken sliced open her cheek. Brushing her finger across her cheekbone, the queen regarded the pool of blood on her fingertip. "Here, I didn't think you had it in you." She smirked. "Obviously, I was wrong. Now that we've established the rules, maybe we should, as you might put it, take off the training wheels."

"Bring it on." The fight continued between the two of them, each hurling one shot after another, dodging, parrying, and volleying all over again. Monitoring the scorch marks or cracks wasn't on her agenda. Those only happened when they hadn't caused the other to stumble back. Only a few steps here and there, but that was okay. This battle was all about timing.

And a misstep was the queen's undoing.

A rapid succession of kinetic arrows, followed by spears, knocked the female flat on her back. As Alicia went invisible, she conjured various spectacles—a collection of stars, a flock of birds, a kaleidoscope of butterflies—misleading her location. She darted across the room, closing the short distance between them, removed the vial of *stupefacient*, dumped the powder into her palm, and blew it into the queen's face.

The female had barely scrambled to her feet before the fine iridescent particles curled in her nostrils. Lurching backward, the queen threw out a hand, slipped against the column, and collapsed to the smooth polished floor.

Without hesitation, Alicia materialized, reclaiming her corporeal form, and tore the heart-shaped sterling silver key from the Red Queen's choker. Footsteps shuffling along reached her ears. Her head jerked toward the sound. Her first instinct was to rush over to Lewis, throw her arms around him, and kiss the ever-living shit out of him. The second—toss him a healing potion, given the inordinate number of slices all over his body. Instead of either, she chose option three. "What do you say we get out of here?"

"Lead the way." With him consistently watching their backs, they hit the corridor behind the thick drapes.

The pulsating energy was like a beacon calling out to her, telling her exactly where to go. She inserted the key into the silver lock, eyeing both directions of the hall. The door swung open wide, revealing a small, mostly empty ballroom. An altar with a glass case atop it sat in the center of the room. *That has to be it.* "Come on, let's go."

Lewis' hand shot out, gripping her forearm. "Let me look first. Make sure it's all clear."

"We don't have time. That stunning powder won't last long." The more powerful the witch, the less effective that shit was. At least in their world. In Wonder… who knew?

"Fine," he said through gritted teeth.

Yeah, yeah. Bitch about it later. Once they were safely back in their own world. Then, and only then, they could unpack all the shit that had happened over the last few days. Marching right up to the altar, Alicia exchanged the key for the athame and spent a good minute studying the glass case. In case of any surprises.

It seemed safe. Safe enough. She glanced at Lewis, who lingered beside her. He nodded, encouraging her to get on with it. As she removed the transparent box, exposing the still-beating heart, the Red Queen appeared at the ballroom's entrance with a half-crazed look on her face. "You bitch!"

"Not the first time I've heard that." Alicia hauled the steel blade high over her head.

"No!" the Red Queen screamed, reaching and lunging toward them as Alicia pierced the heart, digging the blade into that thump-thump.

A luminescent doorway emerged behind her and Lewis. On the other side of it, she saw flurries of snow falling onto the park's ground. *Home.* No time for words. Yanking the athame free from that muscular organ, Alicia captured Lewis' hand as blood splattered all over them. Together, they raced toward their way home. The beating of the heart slowly faded as a set of feet slapped against the floor, trailing behind them. The sole of her boot crunched a bit of ice when they hit some resistance.

The Red Queen had a firm grip on Lewis' ankle. Grunting, he struggled against her hold. They were not fucking going out like this. Alicia conjured a long blade of blood and chopped off the Red Queen's hand. In a comingled mess of limbs, Alicia and Lewis tumbled through the door, landing hard on the snow-covered grass.

The last thing she saw—a flash of red light.

CHAPTER
fifteen

"DON'T RING IT AGAIN."

Yes, they had arrived late, but that was no excuse for the door to have gone unanswered after two rings. Glowering at her twin, Ruby depressed the ivory button a third time. She would damned well do as she pleased. Her sister knew that.

"It's not proper," Rain meekly added.

Nothing about her was proper. Save maybe her dress. Even that was a stretch. Her blood-red corset was a staple in her wardrobe. It perfectly complemented the black silk hugging her legs with a slit up to her thigh. She could hear their mother's words now. *Ladies don't wear tight clothes. A lady's attire shan't be revealing. A lady speaks properly and does not curse.* And on and on. Her twin fit the bill of 'lady' more than she did. That didn't consider her… predilections.

She tapped the toe of her stiletto against the cobbled brick. If that door didn't open in the next two seconds, she'd just walk right in. They were family. Ruby reached toward the knob as the thick oak door swung wide. The butler bowed his head at them. "My apologies, Miss Cromwell and Miss Cromwell. I did not hear the bell."

"No fucking shit," Ruby mumbled, storming in past the male. It was a pathetic—what the fuck? The party room was completely empty. No guests loitered about, gossiping about the couple and their impending ceremony. There weren't any champagne flutes scattered around the room. Stepping farther into the hall, she threw her senses out and got a whole lot of nothing coming back at her. Nada. No wait. A few magical entities gathered on the second floor. She spun around, facing the butler. "What the hell happened?"

"Ruby, that's not our place to inquire," Rain stated.

"Answer the fucking question, Frederick. What the hell happened?" It was bad enough that she and her twin left one clusterfuck behind. Something that was tomorrow's problem. Whatever went down here, it was their prerogative. This was family. They took care of their own.

"My apologies, Miss Cromwell, but perhaps you should speak with the master regarding… um… the issue."

Damn fucking proper shit. "Fine," she snapped. Turning on her heel, Ruby marched up the gilded staircase. The thick carpet silenced her steps. Although she heard her twin calling her name as the female trailed behind her, she didn't stop. Something went down at what was supposed to be a celebration. She'd damned well find out what.

Without knocking, Ruby burst into her uncle's office. She studiously ignored the male gaze that snapped in her direction, focusing solely on her uncle, who stood tense and seething behind his lofty desk. "What happened, Uncle Victor?"

"Your cousin has been missing for a few hours," he replied gruffly.

"Why the hell didn't you call me? I would've found her—"

"And she took that damn egg with her." His eyes narrowed at her as he interrupted her.

Her gaze shot to the empty spot on the mantel. The enchanted item their grandmother had gifted the female on Yule. Why take that? Sensing her twin stop behind her, Ruby shook her head. They should've fucking called. Not that it would've mattered if they had. Both she and her twin had shut their cell phones off. No one in their family needed to know what they'd gotten pulled into earlier. Or still needed to deal with.

The hidden door to the underground passage parted with a soft hiss. Her grandmother exited, joining them. "The family grimoire is missing."

Now it all made sense. Staring at her grandmother, Ruby folded her arms across her chest as she cocked a hip to the side. "You don't think she'd attempt to break that enchantment by herself, do you?"

"She has thought of nothing else since I gifted it to her." The woman pinched the bridge of her nose. "After everything I have done to protect this family," she muttered. Her grandmother's eyes darkened. "We need to find her. Now."

"I've been saying that for the last two fucking hours. I'm so glad you're all on the same page."

While she noticed another male presence in the room, she hadn't taken him in until now. Ruby sucked in a breath. He was *hot.* And deliciously sinful. Biting her bottom lip, she raked her eyes over him. Trimmed, ebony-black hair. Dark, shark-like eyes with obscured emotions swirling beneath the emerald-green irises. Rage twisted his pouty mouth into a sneer. Something she'd happily toy with until that large muscular body of his begged her for mercy.

The loud crack of fingers snapping drew her attention to her uncle. "Ruby! Did you hear me?"

Every fucking word. She was damn good at multi-tasking. Given her uncle's reaction, the male was off-limits. Likely her cousin's intended. Too bad. Breaking him would be a challenge she'd enjoy. "Yes, Uncle Victor. I'll track her down and bring her home."

"Rain, you come with me," her grandmother stated. The woman jabbed a finger at their uncle, daring the male to argue with her. Not that he did.

As her twin left with their grandmother, Ruby crossed over to the oversized Chesterfield armchair her uncle often used. She glanced over her shoulder at the black-haired male as he followed her. "Tracking is a one-person job."

"I gathered as much." He smirked. "Once you've located my fiancée, I'll accompany you on the retrieval."

Excuse me? Fiancée or not, she didn't require help. Facing him, Ruby clasped her hands in front of her body. "*Also* a one-person job."

His green gaze darkened. "And my fiancée needs a lesson in proper party etiquette. That's not in your purview."

Lesson? The only lesson she was prepared to deliver was to this male. Jutting her chin, she stepped closer to him. "And I don't require a babysitter. Your assistance is unnecessary. I can resolve the situation on my own."

"Take Heath with you, Ruby," her uncle called out before they could argue further. Which was fortunate for Heath.

"Fine," she snapped. Closing the distance between them, she glowered at the male. "Just don't get in my way."

Groaning, Lewis rolled over onto his back. The frigid patch of grass dug into his skin as his breaths rose in great puffs. "Jesus Christ." He noticed next to nothing when he peered through that doorway. Except that it looked nothing like Wonder. As his lungs constricted and he shivered, he clearly saw the white particles showering down on them. A New York City winter. Something he hadn't missed.

"You need to get dressed." Alicia shoved a set of his clothes against his pecs. "And then we should leave here."

Clutching his clothes, he pushed against the cold, hard ground and sat up. "Where the fuck are we? Besides home." He quickly tugged his tunic over his head. It wouldn't offer much protection against the harsh wind, but it was better than nothing.

"Central Park. Close to the North Woods."

Fuck. He hoped they weren't anywhere near shifter territory. Maybe it was close to a witch holiday. They monitored those for their own safety. As he got to his feet, he looked up at the night sky and studied the circular shape of the moon. Aside from a small sliver, it appeared full. Jerking his pants up his legs, His gaze dropped to Alicia. "What's the date?"

"Well… it was January 17th when I left." She surveyed their surroundings. "It doesn't look like much time has passed, so it might still be."

"The year?" Christ. It didn't occur to him before now to even ask her that. The days and nights had blended together so much in Wonder, he didn't once consider how to determine the true passage of time.

"Um… 2018."

The hold he had on his pants loosened, his arms falling to his sides. He couldn't have heard her correctly. "What?" he breathed. That couldn't be right. Except she repeated the same year she just gave him. Lewis listed to the right, Alicia caught him, her arms wrapping around him tightly. "I've been gone a year. A fucking year."

"You thought it was longer, didn't you?" she whispered, molding her body to his, warming him from the inside out.

"Yeah." What else could he say? He'd never gone into details with her, but he'd alluded a few times that he'd spent an immeasurable amount of time in Wonder. The passage of time was different. He just didn't think it was anything like this.

"And you're out now. You're free. We're here together. No matter what happens… whatever you need, I've got you. Okay?"

Her eyes locked on his. The spark in those sapphire blues spoke volumes. They gave her words weight beyond their simplicity, calming the tension that swirled inside of him. She was right. He was free. For the first time in a long time, he saw the world clearly. Lewis caressed her cheek with the back of his knuckles. "When you repeatedly fail at something, it's nearly impossible not to give up. You could've left me behind so many times, but you never turned your back on me. Not once. Nor did you let me quit. You didn't just rescue me from Wonder, Alicia. You saved me from myself."

"I'd do it all again. Without hesitation. I may not have known who you were, but I've always known of your existence." The corners of her mouth upturned into a beaming smile. "I just didn't believe you were real."

"Oh, I'm definitely real." Lewis kissed her softly on the lips. With a low growl, he grabbed her by the waist and crushed her body to his. "And you're *all* mine."

"Mmm, *all* yours." Alicia slipped her hands over his shoulders. "Now, what do you say you finish getting dressed and I take you back to my place?"

Oh, he could so get on board with that. "That sounds like a damn good plan." Because all he could think about was getting her naked. Everything else, well, tomorrow was another day.

"This is where she lives." Heath pointed to the storefront of an occult shop. At least if he went by the slew of mystical items he saw in the window display—tarot cards, dream catchers, and more. The shop's name offered no hints. "The Midnight Chesire," he read off the door. "Please tell me this is some kind of joke. A prank. Because I'd believe it."

"Well, technically, her apartment is above the shop. So, no joke." Ruby's face scrunched in amusement.

Heath scowled. He didn't know what to think of this woman. Impressed by her sheer talent. Hungry for the power she possessed. Or irritated by her incessant defiance. The yearning he had to teach his so-called fiancée a lesson didn't compare to the desire he had to bend Ruby over his knee and spank the shit out of that ass. Something he'd never act on. *She doesn't belong to me.* "Then let's get on with it," he seethed.

"I'll move at my own damn leisure. Remember, you're *only* along for the ride."

Before he even realized what he'd done, he'd closed the space between them and wrapped a hand around her graceful neck, stroking his thumb up and down her throat.

"Go ahead," she challenged. "Do it." As a visible tightness settled in her jaw, her pulse quickened.

Fuck him. He'd never faced a female like her before. The throbbing under her delicate flesh socked him in the gut, knocking the air out of him. Even a slight change in pressure around her nape didn't convince her to budge. Her green gaze held strong. This woman bowed down to no one. Releasing her neck, Heath forced his feet back. "Can we please go?" he spat out through gritted teeth.

"Better. Much better." Sashaying forward, the heels of her stilettos clacked against the concrete. She strode past him, stopping in front of a glass door. A small metal box hung on the brick building, denoting three apartments. Ruby gave the glass door a gentle tug. It swung outward, giving them passage.

The stench of hard water and stale cigarette smoke assaulted his nostrils as they made their way up the stairwell. "Good Lilith. How does Victor allow her to live here?"

"If you believe you hold dominion over Alicia just because my uncle promised her to you, then you have another think coming." Her hips swayed with each step she took, climbing the stairs to the second floor. At the top of the landing, Ruby hooked a left.

"That is how it typically works." Though it reaffirmed his suspicions. Victor had lied to him regarding Alicia's etiquette, as well as her powers. Which made it even more necessary to get her in line. They had certain expectations and duties to fulfill. He trailed after Ruby as she approached an apartment hanging off to her right side. He'd lean against the wall, except the yellowed paint had peeled in several places.

Balling up her fist, she pounded on a heavy door. "Alicia!" the female hollered. "It's Ruby. Open up."

"Just a second."

"Why not?" Like they hadn't spent a chunk of the night waiting on her as it was. Between the time Ruby had spent tracking the female to the time it took them to get here, they'd wasted more than enough. Training her in acceptable social graces would give him great pleasure, especially after all he endured tonight. Minutes ticked by as they camped out in front of his fiancée's front stoop. If he could call it that. Nothing except a plain, sky-blue doormat lay at the door's feet.

The door swung wide. Alicia stood on the other side, panting heavily. "What're you doing here?"

Hearing nothing more of their exchange, Heath flicked his gaze from his fiancée's flushed face to the male who hovered behind her. They both appeared out of breath. Although they were both fully dressed, the top buttons of Alicia's top were undone. And the hint of something he couldn't quite identify lingered in the air. What the fuck was going on? Had they… A low rumble sounded in his chest. Heath lunged at the male, striking him in the jaw.

Dodging the hit, the male returned the blow. His fist connected with Heath's cheek, jerking his head to the side. He hardly noticed the sting or the females screaming around them as they exchanged punches, back and forth, pummeling each other and knocking into shit. Yeah, he'd end up with a few bumps and bruises, but he didn't give a flying fuck. That male touched his fiancée. Alicia belonged to him. No one else. It wasn't until the guy threw a right hook that almost knocked him on his ass that he changed tactics. Heath shot the male with an electrical energy ball, center mass, throwing the guy across the room.

Alicia jumped between them, countering the strike, and throttling Heath. He soared through the air. His momentum stopped short. The lip of the hard marble counter smacked his shoulder. A burning sting lanced through him as a *crack* followed and he fell to the wooden floor, landing on his knees.

"Stay the hell away from him!" Alicia bellowed.

"Fuck." Had she seriously defended that piece of shit? And with a hell of a lot more power than Victor led him to believe. What the fuck just happened? Heath shook his head as he slowly got into a sitting position. "Why the fuck did you just attack me? You're my fiancée! I'm well within my right to go after any male who touches you!"

Her blue gaze narrowed at him. "You have no rights." She peered over her shoulder at the male who'd rebounded and risen to his feet, albeit somewhat unsteadily. The two spoke briefly in hushed tones.

"Excuse me?" Heath paid little attention to their words. Instead, he watched the small physical contact between them. The way Alicia rested a gentle hand on the male's arm and how he caressed her cheek. What the fuck was he seeing?

Refocusing on him, Alicia straightened, appearing certain neither Heath nor the male behind her would go at one another again. "We've bonded. You know as well as I do that a bonded witch overrides any agreement made between our families."

Bonded? Fucking hell. Betrothed or not, she was right. Calming himself, Heath scrubbed a hand across his face. "How?" He glowered at her, cutting whatever bullshit explanation she intended to throw at him. "Don't even. You disappeared without a fucking word. Now you say you're bonded to this…" Heath gestured to the piece of shit. "If you want me to accept it, then you owe me at least this much."

Carter jolted upright. Immense power surged through her, overriding the fiery agony in her wrist. That little bitch had sliced her hand right off. Her gaze lifted. A blanket of white covered the world around her. Bare trees filled out the surrounding landscape. Lights twinkled on the horizon. "Holy shit," she gasped. It fucking worked.

While she didn't know where in her former home she had ended up, eventually she would recognize something. First things first. Lifting her arm, Carter watched as the flesh morphed, stretched, and grew. With the energy flowing through her, she created a new, fully functioning hand. The anguish branded by that female slowly dissipated. A fiendish grin crossed her face as she wiggled her fingers. The transformation was now complete. Which meant she had other things to accomplish.

"Come. Let us find a place to work. Then we can hunt our prey. Starting with my blood relations," Carter said as she got to her feet. Nothing came back to her. No response—verbal or otherwise. She surveyed her surroundings. Where the fuck was Jaq? He should've ended up somewhere nearby. Except she didn't see him anywhere.

That made no sense. Unless… the male came to before her and left her here. No. Absolutely not. She saw the injuries on the rabbit in the throne room. Though the male hadn't lost a limb, Jaq hadn't gone easy on him, either. Except she expected him to deliver blows much worse than he had. Just because they needed the rabbit alive at the time hadn't meant he needed to be in one piece. Gripping the material of her gown in her palms, Carter started forward.

If they didn't cross paths, then so fucking be it. They escaped Wonder because of her. He hadn't done a damn thing to help. He just took it like the little bitch he was. She hadn't needed him then and she sure as fuck didn't need him now. Stepping over another fallen branch, she tilted her head at the strangeness in front of her. What the hell was this?

Staring at the unmoving sea of black, Carter cautiously pushed the sole of her shoe against it. Solid. Was it… a road? Had they somehow changed colors? Though it wasn't the only difference that occurred over the last few centuries. An insurmountable number of lights illuminated the night sky. It was no longer just the moon or a lantern they had which to see things. Those motionless torches helped her navigate her way out of the park.

Still, one couldn't be too careful. Despite the noticeable changes, her goal remained the same. Find those of her bloodline and kill them all. Something she'd intended to share with Jaq, but she saw no hint he'd arrived in the new world with her. No matter. She awoke alone and could handle the issue at hand without him. Hesitantly, she stepped out onto the dark road.

Satisfied at how well it held, Carter started forward. A yellow pile of metal screeched to a halt, nearly plowing into her. She eyed the piece of machinery. What the fuck was it? Besides, something that moved. A male climbed out of the thing, shaking his fist at her. "Hey idiot! Get out of the road!"

Carter angled her body in his direction. "How dare you speak to me, you insolent rat." Filthy-ass creature. This presented her with an opportunity. A few, actually. Except she only really cared about one.

"Are you fucking kidding me? I'll speak to you any damn way—"

A red blade barreled through his neck, cutting off his head. The male's dome tumbled to the black river, his body crumpling just opposite of where it fell. Crimson stained the road.

"Well, isn't that nice?" Carter chuckled. Oh yes. Her full power was back. She had everything she required to destroy her bloodline, guaranteeing no one ever put her back in that egg again.

CHAPTER
sixteen

ALICIA STOOD THERE in silence as Heath and Ruby gawked at her. She had recounted the entire story, including all that occurred in the park, glossing over the more intimate parts between her and Lewis. They didn't need those details. At some point, Lewis' hand rested on the small of her back. It gave her all the courage she required to spill it all without fear of what came next.

"So…" Ruby cleared her throat. "All of this…" her cousin gestured to Alicia and Lewis. "That happened because of…" the female's words trailed off. "I'm sorry. It just sounds—"

"Crazy," Heath stated, cutting Ruby off.

"Well, yeah. What he said." Propping her hands on her hips, Ruby pursed her lips. "Do you still have the egg?"

"Yes. It was on the ground in the park when we came through the door. Just as I left it. Like the thing waited on us." She didn't fault either of them for their words or opinions. If she hadn't lived it, she would've thought the same thing. It wasn't the only thing she'd found. The family grimoire, laid out as if it fell from her hands when she disappeared. Not in her satchel where she tucked it safely away prior to their trip into the Red Queen's fortress.

"Let me see it." Her cousin held out her long-manicured fingers for it.

Alicia frowned, almost asking the female *why?* Except when Ruby got that look on her face, there was no arguing with her. Blowing out a heavy breath, Alicia strode over to the couch, dug the yellow crystal Austrian egg out of her satchel, and handed it over. "The enchantment exploded from it after we came through the door." At least she believed that was the red energy she saw.

Her cousin's green eyes narrowed and widened, the whites showing as she scrutinized the egg. Flipping the fastener, she opened the music box, revealing a miniature tea party. At the head of the table sat a pale-faced man with a top hat on his head. Alicia blinked and glanced at Lewis, who'd tensed up. Holy shit. How had she overlooked it? Hell, how had he? Clear as day, the tea party was the one they'd stumbled upon where the Hatter dined with two others.

The tea party went around in circles as music filled the air. A soft ditty, but nothing she recognized. There was something strange about it. Had the air in her apartment thickened? Goosebumps covered her flesh as the hairs on the nape of her neck rose.

"What's wrong?" Lewis asked.

"I don't know." She couldn't place her finger on the sensation or the cause.

"Really? You haven't figured it out?" Ruby's gaze met hers. Before the words left her cousin's mouth, the answer hit Alicia like an unexpected bout of rain in the summer. "The enchantment isn't broken," her cousin stated. "Just subdued. Whatever you did is likely the shift in the air our grandmother felt."

Lewis shook his head. "That isn't possible. She stabbed the heart, just like the spell demanded, and we escaped."

"What spell?" Ruby snapped, closing the music box. "Show me. Assuming you still have the family grimoire."

"I... I... do," Alicia stammered. Another thing she had glossed over—that she lost it for a short time. Swallowing the lump in the back of her throat, she returned to her satchel and produced the thick, leather-bound book. It took no time at all for her to locate the right spell. Although the words had faded, the spell was still legible. Positive she made no mistakes; she also gave the athame to her cousin. "See?"

Ruby's face contorted from acceptance to studious in the flash of a second. "Hmm." Her gaze flicked from the scrawled words to the blade. Then repeated it twice more. Hovering her hand over the frayed pages, the female dragged the blade's edge across her palm without so much as a wince. Droplets of blood fell onto the parchment. It rippled, illuminating something beneath it.

"What the fuck?" No, no, no. This wasn't happening. The spell didn't just alter. Except it did. Her gaze zeroed in on the *one* difference between what they followed and what was now in front of them. It all made sense. The cards caught up to them several times, but caused no actual damage. Then the queen and her fucking taunts. How had she missed it? If that female truly wished for her death, it would've happened. Instead, they played into what the queen desired most.

"It's a false front."

"I don't understand. What does that mean?" When no one answered, Lewis came up behind her, settled a finger under her chin, lifting her face until their eyes met. "Whatever it is, we'll face it together. So, just tell me."

"We set her free," Alicia whispered. There was no other viable explanation. And oh, how she hated those words. She blamed herself for not seeing it sooner. For not being more cautious with the grimoire, especially knowing that it had been out of her possession for at least twenty-four hours.

Lewis grimaced, averting his gaze as he stepped back and paced the length of her living room. He dragged his hand through his brown locks, gripping his hair as if it offered a solution to their situation.

"How the fuck did that happen?" Heath grunted.

Her ex finally got to his feet. Though his gruff question was unwelcome, it gave her thundering heart a chance to settle. "The egg… Wonder…" No matter how she started, none of it felt right. "The Red Queen is of our bloodline. Our faction imprisoned her there. My first night there, I sensed a spell. When I saw the still beating heart on the altar, I used the athame to stab it, setting us free."

"Our bloodline?" Ruby repeated. "Hmm…" Her cousin peered over at her. "While we know you used the wrong weapon… are you sure it was her heart?"

A single line replayed in her mind. *"I've waited a long time for this. Oh, kin of my blood.'"* She thought the comment regarded the spell she had sensed. Could it have meant more than that? Alicia scoffed as the memories of their fight danced in her brain. It had all been so well-orchestrated. Every word carefully chosen. Actions selected with precision. "It was all a ruse. And I fucking fell for it. I'm gonna kill that bitch."

"We have to find this… sword… first," Ruby said.

"No, we don't." Alicia grinned widely. Everything may not have gone according to what she and Lewis planned, but that had. Digging into her satchel once again, she retrieved the sword Lewis had carried on his person from the beginning. Unshrinking it, the weapon reverted to its full size. All that steel gleamed under the lights from her broken lamp.

Lewis halted in his pacing. "We had it the whole fucking time," he said in a breathless whisper. With a smirk, he scrubbed a hand across his face, hung his head, and dropped his hands to his waist. "The whole fucking time I could've killed her."

"Yes, but if you had, I don't know that you would've escaped. It seems that required a bonded witch… from her bloodline." Didn't that make it all that much clearer? Every step she and Lewis had taken together. Was it because they were meant to be? Or just part of some elaborate plan for the Red Queen to escape?

"Right." Blowing out a heavy breath, Lewis frowned as if something flickered across his gray matter. His eyes shot to hers. "Do you think he knew? That he was part of it?"

Fuck. She hadn't considered that. Given what Lewis shared of his fight with the dragon, it played comparably to her fight with the Red Queen. "It's possible."

"We're gonna need help…" Lewis' eyes darted between Ruby and Heath before he continued, "From my pack."

"You're a fucking shifter!" Heath growled. "Are you fucking—?"

"Shut it!" Ruby quipped. "We don't have time to fret about your ego. There are bigger issues at hand."

Although her ex stewed, silence greeted them. Well, well. Wasn't that an interesting development? Not something she intended to toy around with, especially as her own problems arose. "Lewis is right. We're going to need all the help we can get." Alicia slammed the grimoire shut and held it out to her cousin. "Take this back to the house. Fill my father in. And my grandmother. It's best if we summon the whole faction."

"What are you going to do?" Accepting the leather-bound book, Ruby shrunk it down and tucked it away in her tiny black purse.

"I'm going with my mate." Regardless of the questions spinning around in her thoughts, it remained true. "Then we'll go to the source of the egg." Because they made a lot of assumptions. Alicia glanced over at Lewis. The spell may have given them a way out, but she refused to risk everything she found for assumptions.

Especially with all she had to lose.

Lewis traced a finger over the rabbit across the fuel tank of his motorcycle. He couldn't believe his pack held onto it. The thing even appeared well-cared for. The embossment was still as shiny as the day he laid it on all that steel. Had someone ridden it? His gaze dropped to the tattoo of a skeletal figure donning a crown in front of a set of motorcycle handles on his left forearm. No. They wouldn't have done that.

"Hey." Alicia's hand rested on his biceps. "Are you sure you're ready to do this?"

"Yeah." Far from it. There hadn't been enough time for him to re-acclimate to his surroundings. What choice did he have? The Red Queen and her pet were out there somewhere. He wouldn't rest until he buried their ashes in the ground, ten feet under. Capturing Alicia's hand in his, he brought it to his mouth, pressed a kiss to her knuckles, and strolled past the line of hogs.

Together, they rounded the corner. He paused in front of the club's entrance, which should be unlocked, and wiped his palm down his pants. Fuck, he wished he had something better. Not this tunic and leather combo from Wonder. Then maybe he'd feel more in his own skin. Like his old self. But Alicia didn't have any male clothes and this time of morning shops weren't open for business.

"Take however long you need. We don't have to go in right away." Her fingers curled around his arm as she saddled up to him. The warmth of her touch eased the thundering beneath his ribcage. She was both right and wrong at the same time.

Lewis gripped the wooden handle, pulling the door open wide, giving them enough berth to cross the threshold together. Low bass thumped in the background. The clink of balls slamming into one another reached his ears over the din, combined with the yeasty scent of beer filling his nostrils… Fuck. He'd missed this place. This was home. He'd spent the better part of his life inside these walls.

"We're closed," a harsh voice called out without looking in his direction.

"Only to outsiders," he replied. The words came out as if he'd uttered them yesterday. It was like no time had passed at all. At least until the alpha turned from the game of pool and faced him. A blond eyebrow raised over gunmetal eyes. The male lurched toward him, closing the distance between them in several long strides. Before he realized what was happening, a pair of muscular arms came around him in a powerful hug, one that almost cracked his back. Without conscious thought, Lewis released Alicia's hand, returning the embrace.

"Where the hell have you been, brother?" Herak mumbled.

"Long fucking story." One he'd eventually have to recount, but not right now. While they had more important things to discuss, he also didn't have the energy. It was too much for them to delve into all the details that came along with it.

Stepping back, Herak gripped the nape of Lewis' neck. "No matter what it is, you're home." The alpha peered at Alicia, hovering close by, and gestured at her with his chin. "Who's this?"

"My mate." Two words he never thought he'd speak. But he felt them in every part of his soul. That hadn't changed, even with the distance created by that conversation at her apartment. Something they shouldn't have to face yet. Christ. They'd just gotten together. "Alicia, Herak. My alpha. Herak, Alicia." Lewis braced himself in case he needed to take drastic steps to protect his mate. Shifters didn't take kindly to witches.

Herak propped his hands on his hips and nodded to Alicia. "Welcome to the family."

"Um, thank you," she replied.

Lewis' head swiveled back and forth as he glanced between the two of them. *What the fuck?* That was far from the reaction he expected. Snide remarks regarding her species, sure. Jests about him being the first, definitely. An open arm welcome, not a chance. Before he could question anything, another set of enormous arms came around him, squeezing him tight, jerking his feet off the ground.

"Look what the rabbit dragged in," Ewan exclaimed, yukking it up. "Thought ya'd gotten lost in a hole or somethin'."

"Funny," Lewis choked out. At least now he knew who Herak had played pool against. And likely lost. Ewan's hold constricted his lungs, but he didn't give a shit. Hello hypoxia. He'd welcome that shit all day long. It reminded him that he was alive. Almost the same way his mate's touch did.

"I'm jus' glad you're back." The male set him down and clapped him on the shoulder. "I was getting' tired o' takin' care of your hog."

"It's good to see you, too, brother." That was far truer than he dared to express. Although things didn't get all that emotional, the brotherly love in his packmates' eyes was there.

"Hey, Herak," a female voice hollered. A dark-haired beauty stepped out from the hallway. "Think you can…" her words trailed off as her gaze landed on them.

Well. That explained everything and nothing at the same time. His nose wrinkled as the female's briny stench hit his nostrils. A deep growl percolated in his chest as he skillfully tucked Alicia behind him. What the fuck? Talk about one hell of a fucking change.

The female held her palms up and out as if he won a fight they hadn't had. "It's not what you think. I don't hunt like that."

Lewis glowered at his alpha. "A fucking hunter, Herak?"

"And she's under our protection." The male jabbed a finger at him. "So, back off."

Blinking rapidly, Lewis opened his mouth and snapped it shut. The pack was protecting a hunter. He didn't fucking know how to process that. Okay. Some context would help. He rubbed his thumb across his brow. "Why?"

Herak sighed. "You remember the guy that saved my life?"

Something that had only occurred once that he recalled. The alpha usually only took calculated risks after weighing all options. "The fish?"

"Yeah." Herak shot a glare at the female, cutting off whatever objection started coming out of her mouth. Her gaze narrowed as she folded her arms across her chest. But that was her only response. "That's his old lady, Lia. I'm paying back the boon and she's staying with us."

"Got it." He didn't entirely trust those were all the details, but he trusted Herak. The male wouldn't jeopardize the pack's lives.

"He's a merman," Lia retorted, pivoting on the back of her stiletto and storming off down that hallway.

Yep. He knew that. Obviously, the female didn't know about the jokes they all shared after Gray had saved Herak. Maybe she didn't need to. Right.

Ewan snorted a short laugh. "She's a feisty one. Best to look out for 'er."

Something to remember. With that settled, he needed to address the reason for their visit. Lewis wrapped an arm around Alicia, tugging her close to his side. "We need to discuss a situation."

The club door creaked open and shut with a loud clap. A male presence loomed behind him. Lewis didn't even glance over his shoulder before Nasim's voice filled the air. "I'm guessing it has something to do with a witch."

"What makes you say that?" Alicia asked.

Lewis turned, taking in those brooding eyes and that dark hair. Just as he remembered. And the reason he came to the club to begin with. It took a dragon to defeat a dragon. "What she said."

"Because I just saw my past coming back to haunt me."

An answer that said everything and nothing at the same time. Something his pack seemed full of today. Either way, he was certain they'd all jump on board with what he required. That was how their pack rolled—brothers for life.

CHAPTER
seventeen

CARTER STROLLED THROUGH another alley. Defacement and mildew stained the brick wall. Though this one was warmer, likely from the bakery on the other side, than the others that she had checked out. At least the thick scent of yeast masked the foul stench of rotting garbage. How could humans live like this? It was disgusting. If it wasn't for her search, she wouldn't have even bothered with the trek down this back street. But she'd found the perfect place to torture her victims. The only job she had now—find them.

There were two nearby.

Remaining invisible, she readied the stunning powder. It seemed ironic to use something that blonde bitch had used on her, except many witches utilized it back in her day. Plus, her version was much more potent. No reason to chance a witch coming to before she could slap the binding cuffs on whomever she found. Another thing that someone had once used on her.

Why change what worked?

"Grandma, why are we out this way? I thought we were just meant to get the grimoire from your home."

"Hush, child. Your role is merely to offer support, nothing more.

Understood?"

A chill shot down her spine. That voice. It sounded so familiar, but it couldn't be. Her sister would've died centuries ago. That was the cycle of life. It applied to a witch just like any other being. The two magical sources moved in her direction. Stopping in her tracks, she pressed up against the wall and masked her energy signature.

"Yes, Grandmother."

"Good. Now stay alert."

Two females rounded the corner, entering the mouth of the alley, passing a rust-pitted dumpster leaking some unidentifiable liquid. The lack of light offered her little information. From her vantage point, she detected a difference in their hair coloration and age. One had deep-red locks hanging loose, much like her own, and the older female had grayish-blonde hair pinned neatly into a chignon. Something she hadn't seen since she and her sister were young.

"What are we looking for?" the younger female asked.

"Trust me, you'll know it when you see it," the older woman replied. The two moved deeper into the alley, getting closer to her hiding spot. Light from those moving metal boxes washed over the women as it passed by her end of the alleyway. Recognition set in as it illuminated the older woman's face. Same sapphire-blue eyes. Same high cheekbones. The same dainty, little nose.

That hypocritical whore! Carter barely bit back the vile words that threatened to explode out of her mouth. Her jaw clenched as she zeroed in on the other features that belonged solely to her sister. Refusing to wait until those two got within spitting distance, Carter held out her palms and summoned a small breeze. The wind whipped forward, carrying the dust across the air, and showering the two witches with it.

"Plug your nose," Helena screamed, weaving on her feet.

"Grandma?" the younger female said around a coughing fit as she clapped a hand over her mouth. Not that it did either of them a damn bit of good.

Carter stood perfectly still as both women staggered around the alley like a couple of drunk pirates. The knees of the younger gave out within a matter of seconds. Her sister held out longer. Which didn't surprise her in the least. It just meant the female required an extra push. Happily giving it to her, Carter hurled a blast of kinetic energy fused with blood, striking her sister dead center.

It sent Helena soaring through the air. The woman slammed into the dumpster and landed in a pile of dried vomit. Carter stalked forward, pausing long enough to slap a pair of cuffs on the younger witch, and continued on to where her sister lay. Without hesitation, she made herself visible. "Helena. It's been a long time."

Her sister reached a hand out to her. "Carter," the woman gasped, just before passing out.

"Don't worry. There will be plenty of time for us to catch up." Carter cuffed her sister. "Before I kill you." After all, there was no better way to begin her revenge than destroying the woman who started it all.

Alicia opened the door to *Olde Time Trinkets.* The bell chimed above them; alerting workers of their presence as they crossed the threshold. It had killed her to wait until morning, but it gave her and Lewis plenty of time at the motorcycle club. A place they'd spent hours at, where he reconnected with his pack while plans came about regarding their next steps.

"You're certain she's working this morning?"

"I called before we left my apartment." They'd taken his motorcycle. Something she'd never done before. As they walked past a couple of China hutches, she glanced over her shoulder at him. She had hardly taken her eyes off of him since he strode out of her bathroom donning a set of tight leather pants and matching leather jacket over a white t-shirt. When she asked him this morning if that was his normal attire, the growled response said it all.

And then some.

Lewis smirked. "You're staring again."

"I can't help it." Alicia grinned. "I've got a hot-as-sin mate."

"Say that a little louder. Why don't you?"

Like it would matter. No one else was in the store. From what she could see, anyway. And who would care if she shouted it from the rooftops? "Hey. My grandmother told me she's kin. Your kind, not mine."

"Really?" He cocked an eyebrow at her and sniffed the air, grimacing. "Is she… mated?"

"I honestly have no idea. We've never met. Why do you ask?" Her grandmother hadn't shared a lot regarding Grace. Just the basics, she supposed. Alicia ambled farther into the shop, glancing over the various antique items lining the shelves. Some of them reminded her of the things she carried in her own store. Fairies. Mermaids. Phoenixes. Minus a few differences.

"You at least know what she looks like, right?"

"Of course." The website had a picture of a female standing beside an older male, identifying the two as father and daughter. Alicia assumed the woman with light-brown hair was Grace. Since her phone calls to her grandmother went unanswered, it was all she had to go by. Much like the question she posed to her mate a moment ago. Alicia perused an aisle full of music boxes with him in tow. Definitely didn't need one of those.

The female from the photograph bounded toward them. Although this one sported a sparkling diamond ring on her ring finger. Guess that answered the question about a mate. "Hi. Welcome to *Olde Time Trinkets.* Can I help you find something?"

"Grace? Grace Reddington?"

"Yes, that's me." Her eyebrows furrowed as she clasped her hands together. "Do I know you?"

"No, but you know my grandmother. I'm Alicia Cromwell. She purchased a music box from you a couple of months ago."

"Oh, of course. Mrs. Carroll. She's one of my best customers." Grace offered them a polite smile. "What can I do for you?"

"If it's alright with your…" Lewis scanned the empty store and then lowered his voice, "mate, we'd like to speak to you privately regarding the music box."

The corner of Grace's mouth quirked upward. "Except for my mate, we're alone. He's in the back." She hooked a thumb over her shoulder. "He caught your scent before you even waltzed in here and I sensed you the second you entered. We can speak freely. Though, if you feel you need his permission, I'm sure he'd give it. Right, honey?"

Lewis' gaze flicked toward the back hallway. Silence greeted them. His focus not once wavering as if he waited for the permission he sought. Fucking patriarchal society. Was this necessary? Prepared to interject, Alicia opened her mouth—Lewis held up a finger, quietly requesting another second.

"Vincent?" Grace hollered. A grumbled 'fine' came at them. The woman bit back a smirk. "There. So, you had questions?"

"Yes. And I'm just going to be frank. I know that you're a seer. So, it's extremely important that we get whatever information you have." Alicia dug the egg out of her shoulder bag. "Where did you get this? How did you find it?"

Taken aback, her champagne-colored eyes widened. "Oh, wow. I… um…"

Out of her periphery, Alicia spotted a tall male in a four-piece suit step into the back hallway. This wasn't going how she expected. Although Lewis attempted moving her behind him, Alicia wouldn't budge. "I won't apologize for being candid or explain how I know what you are, but I'm not like you. Or human, if that's what you're worried about. Your mate knows what I am. I imagine that's why he didn't come out until now."

"It's fine. I just…" Grace peered back at Vincent. "I promise, I'm fine."

"Good, but I'm not leaving you." Planting his feet firmly, Vincent crossed his arms. "Not until the witch leaves."

Expected, but unwarranted. "I will," Alicia replied. "We will. As soon as we get our answers."

With a nod, Grace blew out a soft breath. "There isn't much I can tell you. I got a vision a day or two after your grandmother approached me. That led me to an auction house." She shrugged. "It took off from there."

"What auction house?" It really wasn't much, but better than nothing.

"Laventhorpe Stronghold Auctions. I've got the address in the back. I can get it for you."

"That would be helpful. Thank you."

"Of course." Grace turned, heading toward the end of the aisle, and stopped. She glanced back at them. "Alicia…" The female's shoulders sagged as if she dishearteningly decided something. "I can't tell you much about the egg, but I can tell you this. It has a dark history."

"Yeah. I can see that." She suspected the female didn't know the half of it. Still, she'd take every piece of intelligence offered. No tidbit was too small.

Carter crouched down on her haunches, staring at the fair-haired female slumped against the brick wall. It should give her great pleasure seeing her sister like this. Passed out. Chained up. Filthy. Except it didn't. She slapped the woman hard across the face, a crack resounding off the walls.

"Stop it!" her other prisoner screamed. "Please," the red-head pleaded. "Just let us go."

"No." Scoffing in pure disgust, Carter rose to her full height of five foot two. Despite having two Cromwell witches in her grasp, including her sister, she got no enjoyment out of it. Though catching them temporarily amused her.

"I'll do whatever you want. Just please let my grandmother go." Her lips trembled as tears rolled down her cheeks.

Good gods. When had witches become so fucking whiny? This female's voice grated on her nerves. "Has anyone ever described you as irritating? Don't get me wrong. Eventually, you'll do what I want, but right now, I need nothing from you, except silence. As for your grandmother, well, I need her to stop playing possum."

"Will it get you to shut up?" her sister groaned.

"No, but that was a good try." It was about damn time. Now, the real fun could begin. Carter crossed the basement, pausing in front of a long wooden table. Eyeing the various tools she'd spread out across her work table, she drummed her fingers against one another. Where to begin? "Tell me, Helena, now that you've stopped feigning sleep, who are all the Cromwells in the area? Or have they extended beyond our fair city?"

"I'm not telling you a damn thing, Carter. Do whatever you plan to do. Nothing will make me talk."

"Yes, of course. I expected as much." Steeling a glimpse of her sister, Carter snickered. Did the female truly believe she was stupid? That she'd torture her first? Instead of the one with no spine. Picking up a pair of pliers, she turned her attention to the other one. "But I imagine your granddaughter will. Tell me, dear, what's your name?"

"Rain," the female replied in a shaky voice.

Oh, fear ran strong in this one. And she hadn't even caused any physical harm yet. "Rain. How precious." Carter took a step toward the young witch. "Tell me, Rain. How many living Cromwells are in the city?"

"Nine," she stammered. "Including my grandmother."

"Shut up!" Helena yelled. "Don't tell her anything, Rain. You keep your trap shut."

Hmm, not too many, but more than she thought. More than she could take out on her own. Not without fighting dirty. Good thing she didn't give a damn about getting in the gutter. It would go quicker if she had help. Damn Jaq for abandoning her. No matter. It wasn't the first time she'd handled shit alone. And getting all she could from young Rain here would set her on the right path. "Don't mind your grandmother. My sister's manners have always lacked. It's perfectly acceptable to answer a question posed by your elder. Right?"

As tears trickled down her face, Rain's green eyes darted from Carter to Helena and back again. The female seemed stuck, like she didn't know which way to go. Or how to proceed.

Oh, this one. Yeah. Like so many others, this witch just needed a little push. "Right, Rain?" Carter dropped the pliers. They hit the table with a dull thud.

Rain flinched. "Right. I mean, um, yes."

"That's fine, dear. Answer any of her questions." Helena let out a short laugh. "It isn't like you know anything of value."

Oh, a challenge. She liked it. Smirking, Carter glanced at her sister. "Are you sure about that? Let's just put that to the test. Shall we, Helena? I mean, they can't all be hypocritical like you. Punishing me for the very magic you used to stay alive and young all these years. Does your family know the truth? Or have you kept it a secret?" Her gaze drifted over the diverse arrangement scattered about for her usage—pliers, hammers, nails, and a variety of others. She picked up the hammer with a rounded edge. "Tell me, Rain. Have the Cromwells expanded beyond New York?"

"I don't know. I mean…" Rain blinked rapidly. Her breaths came out in quick bursts. "I think they have, but I don't…"

Teetering between yes and no. The young woman had the knowledge she required. A little shove would go a long way in getting the bitch to cooperate. Regardless of what Helena said. "Have they?" Carter repeated as she tossed the hammer onto the wooden surface.

"Yes!" Rain blurted. "Into New Jersey."

"You're so weak!" Helena shouted. "I should've drained your magic when I had the chance."

Ah, yes. The truth finally came out. Human sacrifice only went so far. But stealing another witch's power… a devilish grin spread across Carter's face. "That sounds like a marvelous idea." She spared a glance at poor, young Rain. "Don't worry. I won't steal yours. After all, I need someone to draw them all in. Plus, yours won't do much for me." She faced her sister. "You, on the other hand, you'll do wonders. Since I need an army."

Helena scoffed. "No one will serve you."

"I never said they had to be willing." Filled with glee at the path before her, Carter strode toward her sister.

"You can't be serious?" Helena retorted. "Really, sister. Still so predictable… using humans."

"They should be so lucky to serve a purpose. After all, they are tailless rats. Is that not what the vampires call them? Pests. Bugs beneath our feet. Humans are meant to be used at our discretion. *We* are the superior species." With the massive power surging through Helena, she could build the kind of army that didn't die. "Tell me, little one. Where's the closest cemetery?"

"No! I won't tell you that. You can't make me!" Rain shook her head, eyes widening. "We don't desecrate the dead."

Stopping in front of her sister, Carter took one last look at Rain. The horror she was about to force the female to watch would make her completely compliant. That was exactly what she wanted. Because an obedient witch was a powerful tool. "That's where you're wrong. I can do anything I fucking want. And no one can stop me."

Lewis took stock of the bare walls, the faded spots dotting the wallpaper where he imagined art once hung, vacant benches. Though they noticed the auction house appeared abandoned, Alicia had broken into the building. They had to see it all up close for themselves. The emptiness of it all was eerie as fuck. It creeped him out.

"Well, that was a complete bust."

"Maybe not entirely." Aside from the obvious, they learned something significant about the egg.

Alicia gestured to the vast space surrounding them. "Am I missing something?"

"The name." Which had also been removed from the door. They found a single business card on the thin carpet by the receptionist's desk, confirming the location. He rubbed his thumb across his forehead. "Grace called this place 'Laventhorpe Stronghold Auctions,' right?"

"Yeah. So?"

"The Red Queen's castle has the same name. If I had to take a guess…
I'd say that somehow, she controlled the movement of the egg." It would
explain how it landed in his possession, eventually finding its way to
Alicia. Only the gods knew where else it ended up.

"Maybe."

"Hey." Forgetting all about the empty space, he brushed the back of his
knuckles across Alicia's cheek. "What's going on? Talk to me. You've been
distant since last night."

She flashed him a tight smile. "You noticed that, huh?"

"Yeah." And he had given her space to reach out on her terms. They'd
had little time to celebrate their victory before it all blew up in their faces.
Something neither of them addressed.

"I don't know," Alicia sighed. Backing up a step, she walked a slow circle
around the room. Her way of collecting her thoughts. "Do you believe
in destiny? Fate?" She shot a glance his way. "I keep thinking about that
spell. And the Red Queen's involvement in everything. How much of it
did she control? How much was in our control? If she needed a bonded
witch to escape, then does that mean we were destined to be together? Or
did we choose that? And she just got lucky?"

"Why can't both be true?" Before her, fate was the journey you took to
get from point A, birth, to point B, death. Nothing more. Meeting her
changed how he viewed life and love. It didn't mean things would be easy
for them. They'd get judgment from both of their species. None of that
altered how he felt.

Alicia halted in her tracks. Her eyebrows pinched together as she gaped
at him. "But how?"

"I believe we were destined to meet. Our fates were intertwined. The
Red Queen didn't control that. She merely set up the circumstances. But
the rest… trust, respect, love… that was our choice. No one made that
for us. Not the gods or the Red Queen. That belongs to us. We own that."
With each word he spoke, he closed the distance between them. The spell

might have forced them together, but they constantly chose one another over anyone else, including themselves. He would risk death for her. Just as she'd do for him.

Her sapphire blues sparkled beneath the low lights. "Love?"

"Yeah. Love." Lewis planted his hands around her waist, drawing her body against his. "Because I love you, Alicia. Never think otherwise."

"I love you, too," she beamed up at him.

With a low rumble of approval, he fused their lips together, hungrily devouring her mouth. Her exquisite scent flared in his nostrils, sending a blaze across his nerve-endings. Fuck. He didn't know if he could wait to get her home. Out of nowhere, a song blasted around them, breaking the moment. "Don't answer that," he growled. Whoever the fuck it was could call back.

Later.

Alicia dropped her forehead to his chest. "I have to. It's Ruby."

"Alright." Like he could argue with that.

Digging the phone out of the back pocket of her jeans, Alicia pressed it to her ear and answered the call. "Hello?"

"Hey, it's me. Have you talked to Grandma today?"

"No. I've left a few messages, but haven't heard from her yet."

"What about Rain?"

"No," Alicia drew out the word as she lifted her head. "Why? What's going on?"

"Rain didn't come home last night. And Grandma never returned to Uncle Victor's. No one else has seen or heard from them in hours."

None of this sounded good. Listening to both sides of the conversation, Lewis ran his fingers up and down Alicia's spine. Her pulse quickened throughout the call.

"Have you tried tracking them?"

"Yes. And I get nothing." Ruby paused. "I can't find them."

His gaze slipped around the empty building and his eyes drifted shut. Shit. No fucking way. This wasn't happening.

"The Red Queen," Alicia whispered.

"Are you trying to tell me that psycho bitch has my sister?" Ruby exclaimed.

"We're heading your way now. We'll find them, Ruby. I promise you."

Of that, the female could be sure. Lewis captured Alicia's hand in his own, giving it a gentle squeeze as they made their way toward the exit. It was beyond time they ended this cycle with the Red Queen.

CHAPTER
eighteen

"THERE ARE TWO heat signatures," Lia stated as she came around the corner.

Ruby nodded. This was good. It gave her hope that her twin was alive. Not that it stopped her from asking for more. "Could you tell who they belonged to?"

"No, but I found a way in."

"Good. Now head back to the club," Herak stated.

"Absolutely not. I will not hang out there while all of you are out here fighting. Especially when I can help." As if to prove her point, Lia rechecked the myriad of weapons she strapped across her body.

"Just do as I say," Herak snarled.

Lia glanced at her like this argument irritated her. Which made two of them. "You're not the boss of me," Lia retorted. "So, stop fighting with me on this."

"It's my job to protect you. And the safest place is the club."

"Then stick someone from the pack on me because I'm not going anywhere."

Christ. If she had to listen to another word between the two of them, she'd slap them both. "Just let her stay," Ruby said. Aside from the fact Lia was one of the few people she trusted, they covered a multitude of bases this way—hunter, shifters, and witches.

Herak pinched the bridge of his nose. "Fine. Then you're on the rescue op with Ruby, Heath, and Ewan."

"That's bullshit."

"Lia." Ruby glowered at the female. They were doing nothing except wasting time. This didn't help the situation, which was already bleak. They'd accomplish more with teamwork.

Without a word, the female raised her hands in defeat.

Finally. Dipping her chin to the three joining her, they splintered off from the primary group. "Lead the way." Ruby gestured to Lia. Together, they moved through the alley as a four-star unit heading toward an abandoned building. Lia claimed the front position, while the two males flanked her, and Ruby took the rear. Despite all their efforts, their tracking hadn't led them beyond the abandoned building. They hadn't even been able to confirm Rain and their grandmother lived.

Nor had they found the Red Queen.

Which was why most of the group stayed outside. They didn't know a damn thing about what they walked into. With their grandmother missing, they had even less knowledge regarding the Red Queen's true power. Alicia's insights gave them little to go on.

Lia stopped in front of a metal grate. "This is our access point. It leads right into that building."

Eyeing the entrance, Ruby raised an eyebrow at her friend. "What is it with you and sewers?" Hadn't they just done this? She frowned as the days replayed in her mind. Gods, yeah. Less than a week earlier.

"Afraid you're going to ruin your Jimmy Choo's?" Lia remarked.

"Louboutin's," Ruby corrected. "And no." Her twin was worth far more than a pair of fucking shoes. *Fuck me.* "Let's get it up."

It took little effort for Ewan to lift the framework, giving them entrance to the underground tunnels. They held true to their formation, climbing down the cold iron rungs of the ladder. As they trudged through waterlogged garbage, stepping around a variety of debris, Ruby surveyed the curved cement walls ahead and backward.

"Waiting for something to jump out?" Heath called over his shoulder.

"Maybe." Preparation for every possibility hurt no one. The more she checked things out, the better prepared she was for whatever came her way. Albeit, she couldn't predict or prepare for everything.

"I don't hear anythin' 'cept for some rats," Ewan said.

"Better than the alternative." There was no telling what traps that psycho laid out for them. Regardless of her efforts, she'd defer to the shifter. His hearing was better. As was his eyesight. Silence stretched between them as they made their trip. They'd just reached the end. Something sloshed behind her. Ruby peered over her shoulder, straining in the darkness to determine the cause.

Nothing.

It had to be her imagination. Fuck, she was losing her mind. Ruby ascended the ladder right behind Heath. As she popped up into the building's skeletal silhouette, she found him holding his hand out to her. Without accepting the offered palm, she eyed the once vibrant façade marred by peeling paint and cracked plaster. Where in this hollowed interior was her family stowed?

"This way," Lia said, leading them deeper into the maze of darkened rooms.

As they strode past wooden doors hanging on rusted hinges, she couldn't help but notice the tattered furniture and scattered debris. A chilly breeze swept through the corridor, serving as another reminder that the building slowly succumbed to the relentless embrace of nature. Or that something dark lurked in the shadows.

A soft groan echoed from a room a few yards ahead. Her heart thundered in her chest at the noise. It wasn't much, but she knew who it belonged to. Shoving Heath and Ewan aside, Ruby plowed ahead. She burst into an underlit space. The musty scent of decay slammed into her. Gods, it smelled—"Holy shit."

On one side of the room, a female with the same hair color as her grandmother and shrunken cheeks lay slumped and chained to the brick wall. She didn't have time to register what she saw when she spotted her sister crumpled on the ground on the other side. Lines of tears streaked the female's face. Not that Rain cried. Rasping breaths escaped her twin's mouth.

Ruby rushed over, dropped to her knees, and studied the cuffs locked onto her sister's wrists. "Rain?" she called. "Can you hear me?"

"I'm so sorry. I tried…" the female rambled. "I tried not to tell her. But I had to. I had to," she sobbed.

"Tell her what?" What the fuck was her sister going on about? Had the Red Queen wanted to know something? Was that why…? Shit… she couldn't think about that right now. Ruby yanked the thick links through the metal loop. Although she got her twin unchained, how the fuck was she supposed to unlock the cuffs? They didn't have a hole for a key. Or a place to insert a combination.

"I'm sorry," Rain repeated. "I'm sorry. She made me."

"Shh, it's okay. It's—" The sounds of groans and shuffling feet approaching cut her off. Ruby lifted her gaze, locking on the closest person: Ewan.

"We've got company!" he hollered.

"Fuck!" Heath yelled. "It's a walking dead spell. They're zombified."

Son of a bitch. That damn psycho witch. She knew she'd heard something. "They're human," Ruby screamed. "We can't kill them." All they could do was knock them out repetitively until the spell broke. Or the queen died. Whichever came first. Hopefully the latter, depending on how the group outside fared.

"It keeps getting back up!"

"Then cut off its head! It's already dead."

"Not all of them," Alicia corrected. They'd spent the better part of the last ten minutes or longer fighting zombies. For a lack of a better word. Fucking necromancy. The bane of a blood witch's pedigree. It was forbidden to raise the dead. Obviously, that wasn't out of line for the Red Queen. That, combined with the humans under the female's control, spelled a lot of fucking trouble.

Either way, they couldn't keep this up forever.

Something had to give.

From the corner of her eye, she sighted a magnificent scaled beast with a wide-open maw soaring through the air. Alicia decked the human she faced off against, knocking it back on its ass. "Holy shit." *Lilith, please don't let that be Nasim.* Or let him do something stupid.

The creature unleashed a torrent of searing, vibrant flames from its mouth. The flames danced and twisted like a liquid inferno as they shot out, setting a host of dead bodies on fire. Heat radiated from its breath, visibly distorting the air. Flying overhead, it swooped down and landed several yards away on the desolate expanse of cracked asphalt.

Alicia watched as the dragon shifted, transforming back into the dark-haired male she'd met yesterday. "Fuck," she groaned, dragging a hand down her face. They had yet to see the Red Queen. Instead, they faced an endless supply of a conjured army. She jogged toward the male, striking out against the enemy along the way. "Nasim!"

As he approached, he ripped the head off of a mostly decomposed corpse. His gaze flipped to her. "Tell me I didn't get any of the wrong ones."

"No. I don't think so." Though she wasn't sure. Alicia scrutinized the various fighting pairs. Shifters and witches alike battled zombies and the walking dead. Of those bodies writhing on the ground from the flames, they all appeared—her eyes narrowed, focusing on her father.

He swung a blood sword, bringing it down in an arc, but against what? She saw nothing. No. That wasn't accurate. Something knocked him back. His steps swaggered as an invisible force struck him. The blade fell from his hand, disappearing into the pavement without so much as a sound.

What the hell? Eyes bulging, Alicia raced toward the fight. Her feet pounded against the concrete, slapping with each step she took.

Her father's body lifted, hanging there like in suspended animation.

The tips of his leather oxfords barely touched the weeds pushing through the pavement cracks. His arms stretched out as tension claimed every limb. With his mouth open wide, something rippled between him and the invisible force.

Alicia screamed as his cheeks slowly shrunk, becoming unrecognizable. His skin shriveled, the bones transforming into something visible beneath his flesh. It was as if someone sucked the life force right out of him, leaving him as nothing more than a shell of a man. A pair of muscular arms came around her as her father's lifeless body crumpled to the ground. Tears streamed down her face as she sobbed in utter anguish.

"Stop," Lewis pleaded quietly in her ear. "You can't help him. There's nothing you can do."

A cackle swirled around them as a current of electricity undulated. "Who's next?" Where nothing once stood, the Red Queen appeared, pointing her long, blood-red nails at the witches, one by one. "You? Perhaps you?"

Her mother and sister each lobbed a spell at the female. Red stars rained down, slicing the queen's flesh, as a ring of fire erupted around her. Flames licked at the woman, singing the hair on her arm. Exploding in laughter, she quashed the blaze and redirected the stars.

Fuck. No, no, no, no. Alicia struggled against her mate's hold. "You have to let me go! I can't lose them!" She swallowed the lump in the back of her throat, desperately clawing against an overwhelming flood of emotions that threatened to unleash inside of her.

"Not alone. We fight together. Remember?"

It was what they agreed. That no matter what happened, they'd fight side-by-side. With a slight nod of her head, she whispered, "I remember."

"Then let's go get the bitch."

As he released her, the two of them ran head first into the fight. Not that her mother and sister had stopped their assaults. They alternated, back and forth, forcing the Red Queen to defend against the both of them. Alicia and Lewis easily jumped in, adding fuel to the fire. While he struck at her with his sword, Alicia, her mother, and sister worked together, switching up the magic they threw. They interchanged the type and timing, pulling the queen's attention in several directions at once.

All they had to do was distract her until Lewis pierced her heart. Then it would all be over.

A potent kinetic force billowed out of the queen. All four of them flew, thrown into the air, their bodies colliding with the asphalt with a loud thud. Lewis' sword skittered across the ground. Alicia groaned at the jarring jolt that speared her shoulder.

"Did you really think that would work?" the queen taunted. "That you could defeat me? You can't! I'm far too—" A gleaming tip of silver poked out of her chest, cutting off her words. The queen's features paled as she hiccupped blood, crimson dribbling down her chin.

What the hell? Had Lewis gotten to his feet? She couldn't tell for sure. Pressing her hands against the pavement, Alicia pushed herself into an upright position. Her shoulder hollered at her. Motherfucker.

"You're nothing," a dark-haired male drawled as he thrust the sword deeper into the queen's chest cavity.

Alicia blinked. It couldn't be. But that voice… she only heard it once while she and Lewis hid in a teapot. Was that… what had he called the guy? The knave?

The queen's fingers curled against her chest as she collapsed. "Jaq," she gasped. "Why?"

Whatever the reason, the male offered her nothing. He simply stood there, his eyes cold, as blood pooled beneath the queen's body. Alicia watched as her sister, mother, and Lewis scrambled to their feet. Her mate joined her side as the Red Queen took her final breath.

The male's hard stare roamed over those gathered, stopping on Nasim. "Brother," Jaq said. Without another word, Jaq backed up several steps and shifted into a massive black-scaled dragon. His slitted eyes glared at all of them, forcing each shifter and witch to give him a wide berth. With a deep, guttural roar, he breathed a stream of fire at the queen's remains. Almost as if the male refused the chance that she returned to life. As the flames licked at her flesh, turning the queen into a pile of ash, he pivoted and disappeared into the night sky.

A pulse of energy rippled outward, releasing the control the queen had claimed of the gathered corpses and humans alike. As the dead bodies dropped to the ground like nothing more than litter scattered around the empty lot, the living came around. Confusion contorted their faces. Although the Red Queen's death relinquished the spell over them, there was one that remained.

Alicia flicked her gaze toward her father's shriveled-up body. Her mother and sister hugged one another, quietly sobbing. Lewis' arm wrapped around her waist, drawing her against him. Releasing a heavy breath, Alicia pressed her head to his pec. Silent tears rolled down her cheeks. No words could ease her pain. She may not have gotten along with her father, but she still loved him.

And now he was gone.

Across the way, a metal door clanged. Ruby limped out, hugging her twin sister to her side. Heath, Lia, and Ewan exited the building's shell behind her. Whatever they had faced inside the building had been just as brutal as outside it. Similar to everyone there, they all looked a little worse for wear. There was one person she didn't see among the gaggle. Alicia locked eyes with her cousin. Ruby simply shook her head.

Yes, they had won, but they had lost, too.

In the remnants of a hard-fought battle, it seemed as if they had lost too much. That innate desire to break the egg's enchantment had caused all of this. Was it worth it? Glancing around at all the faces, Alicia realized they had gained something as well. Not just family, but a better understanding and respect for their individual species. Never in their history had shifters, witches, and a hunter come together.

The first of the sun's rays filtered over the horizon, marking the dawn of a new day.

And a better tomorrow.

EPILOGUE
One month later...

"I FEEL LIKE something is missing." Lewis took one last look at his reflection in the full-length mirror. The crimson silk pants and matching long-sleeve top he donned appeared perfectly in place. He adjusted the sash around his waist that held the ceremonial athame, ensuring it sat closer to his hips.

"Stop messing with shit," Herak said. "This is exactly how they told me you should look."

"Are you sure?" He glanced over his shoulder at his alpha. Yeah, it seemed like a dumb question. Ruby had shown up at the clubhouse several times, covering every aspect of the ceremony, front to back. And not just with him. Although she was no longer on the market, his pack adored the female. Or they feared her. He hadn't quite figured out which.

"Yes, I promise."

"How do you know?"

"Because I have pictures."

His brows furrowed as he spun around, facing the male. "Pictures? As in colorful photographs of other guys who *look* like me?"

"Yuk it up, you ass. Ruby provided me examples." Herak shook his head. "Shithead."

"Everyone has a calling in life." He cracked a grin, chuckling at the male. While his pack didn't touch his room the whole time he'd been gone, he'd never moved back into it. It seemed wrong to spend his nights anywhere but next to his mate. Plus, things were different now. Not just because he had Alicia, but because the dynamic with his packmates had changed. Although his disappearance had been nothing more than a year for them, for him, it had been nearly twenty. He was still figuring out how to handle that… discrepancy. Among other things. Even with the Red Queen dead, he still had demons to face.

Herak clapped him on the shoulder. "Seriously though. I'm glad I'm here for this."

"And that I'm the first lucky bastard?" Lewis cocked an eyebrow at his friend. "I mean, we don't have ceremonies like this."

"No, but maybe we should. Something a little more than just tatting her name on our body. Speaking of… have you… talked about that?" The male gestured to his right biceps.

Yeah, the tattoo of a heart with a tilted crown had come up in conversation. Something he'd done based on the dreams he had of Carter before she imprisoned him in Wonder. "Alicia said she understood, that it didn't bother her. Just served as a reminder of all we've endured. Still… I think I'm gonna change it. Make it more than what we've endured. Make it… better."

The door cracked open. Nasim poked his head around the jamb. "You ladies done chatting? It's time."

"When did this become 'pick on Lewis' day?" Every one of his brothers had something sarcastic to say. And he enjoyed every second. Like nothing and everything had changed between them.

Nasim smirked. "You're getting bonded. I feel like that speaks for itself."

"He's got a point," Herak chimed in.

"Fuck you both."

"Thanks, but I'm good. I don't feel like cleaning rabbit fur out of my teeth."

"Fucker," Lewis snickered. He strolled after Herak and Nasim. The three of them left the dressing room together. They stepped into the hall, descended the staircase, and headed toward the ceremonial room. The soft, white rug covering the stairs tickled his bare feet, grounding him. As he hit the bottom step, the rug transformed into white silk. It carried him like a cloud, leading him to where his new life awaited. Approaching the main room, he noted the bright and airy atmosphere. Each white chair had a white bow tied at its base. All the walls had been done in the same color, looking like a blank canvas, naturally reflecting light. From what he learned, it represented new beginnings.

Seated guests turned, watching him as he took his place at the front of the room by the high priestess. Herak and Nasim stood at his flank. Like him, they also wore a set of silky crimson pants and a shirt. With the sash, they all looked like they rocked some fancy PJs. Lewis glanced at the crowd. Each attendee had some version of his attire. Dress or suit, it was all the same color, signifying the union of two bonded souls.

A few of those gathered spoke in hushed tones. He recognized most of them. Over the last month, Alicia introduced him properly to several of her family members. At least the more prominent ones. They all felt the loss of her grandmother and father. While life moved forward, Alicia seemed less inclined to involve herself with faction issues. Something he fully supported.

The room fell quiet. As a whole, the crowd stood. Each person bowed their head, presenting a white rose in their hand. Ruby came around the corner first, followed by Angel. He didn't pay much attention to what they wore. Other than it being red.

But the moment Alicia came into view, she took his breath away. His entire body stilled. Every part of him lit up. Everything around him fell away. Alicia's blonde hair cascaded down her back in loose ringlets. It contrasted the deep red of her gown. The strapless red-sequined lace hugged her curves perfectly, puffing out at her waist. The corset had a deep V, accentuating her cleavage. Gods, she was undeniably stunning.

His eyes never once left her as she walked toward him. It wasn't until she stood before him that he noticed the guests had thrown the white roses at her feet.

"Welcome all," the priestess began. "Today we call upon Lilith, the first of us, and our forefathers as we celebrate the bonding union of Lewis Sheen and Alicia Cromwell."

At that point, the female switched to another language. Latin, he believed, but he couldn't say for sure. There wasn't any kind of verbal response required of him until after they pierced their hands with the athame. Alicia called it a blood communion.

"We ask the goddess Lilith to bless this union. May your words be loving and compassionate. May she fill your days with joy and bounty. May she offer her guidance when it is most needed. In her name, we pierce the body, mind, and soul."

Lewis removed the athame from his sash, pressing the tip of the dagger into the center of his palm. "By piercing the heart of my whole, I, Lewis, accept and claim you, Alicia, as my one true bonded mate."

Once blood welled, he held it out to Alicia for her to do the same. "By piercing the heart of my whole, I, Alicia, accept and claim you, Lewis, as my one true bonded mate." Then she clasped their hands together, palm to palm.

Simultaneously they said, "May we forever be joined until our last days."

The priestess wound a tri-colored rope around their coupled hands, tying it off at their wrists. Black represented his line, red signified her bloodline, and white bound them together. "From this day, henceforth, I proclaim you as one body, one mind, and one soul. You may now kiss your bonded mate."

At that moment, a current of power bloomed between them, thrumming under his flesh. *Holy shit.* His eyes widened. Alicia warned him he would sense the magic flowing in her veins, but this wasn't what he imagined. Staring at her, he saw everything he had missed and hadn't known he needed. Closing the distance between them, Lewis pressed a soft, lingering kiss to Alicia's lips. "I love you," he whispered as everyone around them jumped into an explosion of joyous celebration.

"I love you, too," she replied. Her entire face lit up. Her features unequivocally glowing.

Together, they faced the crowd and strolled down that white-silk path, hand in hand, commemorating their new beginning. He leaned down close to her ear. "How long do we have to hang around here? Because seeing you in that dress… I'm dying to get you out of it." That exquisite scent of her arousal hit his nostrils, drawing a rumble out of him.

"I'll tell you what. I'll make you a deal. Give it an hour. Then we can take our leave. Because once I'm out of this dress, there's no way it's coming back on."

"I like the way you think," Lewis growled. "It's like we really are of one mind."

Alicia beamed at him. Her blue eyes sparkled like sapphires in the light. "Forever and ever."

"All mine. My bonded mate."

The End

ABOUT THE AUTHOR

Author of the Love's Worth Series, BRIGIT ROSÉ lives in a world of romance. She has taken her life experience and made it into one endless love story. When she's not writing, she's singing loudly and off-key, hanging out with friends, or playing with her 2.5 fur babies. She can usually be found with a kiss in one hand and a twist of line in the other, exactly the stories she likes to read and write. If you'd like to know more about Brigit, you can find out more on her website: HTTPS://KBFENNERROSE.COM.

OTHER WORKS BY BRIGIT ROSÉ

LOVE'S WORTH SERIES
UnHinged
ReIgnited

THE MYSTIC CHRONICLES
Detached

THE LUCENT CHRONICLES
Grace's Beast
Shattered Wonderland

THE ARCAREAN ACADEMY
Wicked Ground

Co-authored

PRISMA ISLE SERIES
Perfectly Reckless
Chaotic Tranquility
Rebel Tides

Under Krys Fenner

DARK ROAD SERIES
Addicted
Damaged

Avenged

Burned

Twisted

THE GUARDHIAN SERIES

Awakened

Disillusioned

COMING SOON

Betrayed (Dark Road Series)

ReUnited (Love's Worth Series)

Inherited (The Guardhian Series)

Siren's Curse (Prisma Isle Series)

Silencing the Shape Shifter (Prisma Isle Series)

Kingdom of Embers (Prisma Isle Series)

Darkness Reconciled (Prisma Isle Series)

Savage Ground (The Arcarean Academy)

Consumed (The Mystic Chronicles)

Dark Entanglement (The Midnight Chronicles)